Move the Needle

By Christian Cashelle

Move the Needle
By Christian Cashelle

ISBN-13: 978-0-9894423-9-8
Copyright 2020 @ Dynamic Image Publications

Edited by: Jasmine Clayborn

Manufactured in the United States of America

Other titles by Christian Cashelle

Ava Series
Ava's Story
When All Else Fails
My Mother's Child

Camryn Series
My Joy
Gino's Revenge

Revisions of Life
Birds in the Rain

Visit www.dipublications.com for more.

Move the Needle

One

Approach life just as you approach business; with confidence on your own terms. That was how 27-year-old Sage Anderson had been successful thus far. It may have taken her a while to find her groove, but she was now in the swing of things and creating the life she dreamed of. She may not have had everything on her vision board, but she was content and didn't need anyone else's approval to be so.

"How many times have you heard the saying, 'doing the same thing and expecting different results is insane' yet you still keep doing the same things. It's like your brain hasn't registered that it's time for you to do something new. God wouldn't keep taking you through the same test if you would just learn something."

Sage swiveled around in her gray leather chair with her eyes closed until she felt the sun on her face. She opened her eyes to be greeted by the world outside of her home office window as the sermon played from her laptop. It was true, she had heard that saying about insanity a lot. People posted it all the time and she always wondered if they were actually applying it to their lives. She smiled, knowing that she had. She wouldn't be running her own business if she didn't take that advice.

"Sage Consulting, how may I help you?" she answered her ringing phone. "Yes, I can definitely walk through my services for you, unfortunately I do not provide free consultations."

Sage rolled her eyes as the caller began to make excuses about why she couldn't schedule a consultation. She was used to people flaking on her. It was why she no longer offered free consultations in the first place.

Once the phone call ended, Sage pulled up her website to check and make sure all of her hyperlinks worked. She did this once a week while creating her social media posts for the following week. While she was brainstorming, she got a call from her sister.

"Hey Londra," she said. "You off already?"

"Sis, 3PM and I ran out of there, you hear me?"

Sage laughed. "Well, now you have a free weekend. Enjoy it."

"I will," Alondra said. "Because my sister is going out with me."

Sage frowned. "Who said that?"

Alondra sucked her teeth. "Okay, Porsha," she said. Sage smirked at the reference to their favorite reality television star before her sister started whining. "Come on, Sage! My friends are boring. I wanna hang with my big sister."

Sage sighed. Alondra was twenty-three and proved to be the baby of the family at every turn. She loved her though. She was always a good kid. Alondra was in her last year of undergrad, majoring in criminal justice. There was a time they butted heads growing up, because they were so much alike. Their relationship was strained during their brother's death when Sage was a junior in college. They were just able to repair their relationship within the last couple of years. Sage knew she should be grateful that Alondra wanted to spend time with her now.

"Where are we going?" Sage asked. Alondra squealed and although Sage knew she'd regret it, she was happy that her baby sister even wanted to spend time with her.

"360."

Sage rolled her eyes. There weren't many places in St. Louis that she liked to go to, but she was honestly tired of 360.

"Okay, sis. Let me get back to work. I'll see you tomorrow."

"Love."

Sage did a little more work before deciding to call it a day. She had three consultations set for next week, which was a productive day for her.

She turned off her computer and closed the door to her office on the way out. Stopping in the hallway she admired her shape before poking at her love handles.

"Might as well go to the gym," she groaned.

That was her usual routine. Do her work, try and get some self-care in and come home. Sage tried not to focus on the fact that she was nearing 30, single with no children. She had been content with the direction of her life, but after so many of her college friends began getting married and having children, Sage began to feel the comparison trap creep into her thoughts. Of course, she wanted love. She wanted what her parents used to have. She wanted someone to build a legacy with. It was what she always dreamed of since she was a little girl.

Everything in her life was planned, but after being let down in the love department time and time again, Sage decided to focus on things she could control. Everything else would just have to wait.

The following evening found the Anderson sisters at 360. Although Sage wasn't too excited to attend, the atmosphere that night was nice. In true Midwest fashion, the weather hadn't gotten the memo that it was still February, so all the doors were open and the downtown skyline was beautiful at night. Sage appreciated the air against her neck. She rolled her shoulders a few times to help her relax as Alondra bopped to whatever song was playing. Sage recognized it was a Lloyd record, but she hadn't heard it before.

They sat at the bar under the DJ booth that was suspended in the air. Alondra sat on the end with Sage to the right of her. She crossed her feet at the ankles, tapping her heels against the bar of the stool before looking at her sister's side profile. Alondra was the "big, little sister" as Sage called her often. She was over an inch taller and had a lot more curves than Sage. Their facial features were the same, specifically the nose, but Alondra looked more like their father.

Alondra must have felt Sage looking, because she quickly turned to her with a raised eyebrow.

"You aren't drinking?" she asked, leaning over the bar and smiling at her sister. Sage swayed in her seat to the rhythm of the song. She shook her head and placed both hands flat on the bar top.

"I went to the gym today."

Alondra frowned. "Okay? Means you got calories to spare," she turned towards the bartender. "I'll have a Crown Apple and cranberry and my sister is having…"

Sage sighed. "Dry martini, please."

Alondra sighed dramatically as she sat down. "You're such an old maid."

"Thank you," Sage said, rolling her eyes. "How was class this week?"

"Literally counting down the hours to graduation."

"That's a lot of hours."

"Don't remind me," Alondra bit her lip and gave Sage her innocent look.

"Nope…"

"Come on Sage, you don't even know what I'm going to say."

"If it has anything to do with Daddy, I don't want to hear it."
Deflated, Alondra sank down in her seat and waited for her
drink. Sage sighed, not wanting to fight with her. "Let's just
enjoy our sister night out please? I needed a break, I'll be
honest. Thanks for inviting me."

Alondra slowly smiled. "See? I knew you did."

"You were right," Sage said, smiling at her sister.

"Great, so you won't mind doing a favor for me?"

Sage sighed. "I knew it."

"It's a win-win though," Alondra said, holding both of her
hands up in a mock surrender. "I promise."

Sage sighed, looking around the bar at the people coming in
and out. Sage glanced at her sister and laughed at her
impatient facial expression.

"Stop scrunching your nose that way," Sage said. "You'll get
wrinkles." Alondra rolled her eyes. "What is it, Londra?"

"My line sister, Tiffany, is doing a profile of some business
owners on her blog and she wants to interview you. She's been
getting some traction on her site but she wants to put
something together since March is women's month or
something like that."

"National Women's History Month," Sage corrected.

Alondra waved her hand. "Yeah that...so she wants to profile
local business women and I think you'd be perfect. It's going
to be a little photoshoot and everything. You can get some
headshots and such…"

"What's in it for you?" Sage wondered.

Alondra sighed. "It was more so a barter of sorts, she's
going to help me design my website."

Sage nodded. Alondra had been talking about starting a
website to promote a nonprofit that she wanted to create once
she graduated. It would be a resource in support of children
who have lost someone close to a traumatic event.

"Okay, I'll do it."

"Really?" Alondra stood from the seat to hug her sister. "I really thought you'd say no."

"Why?" Sage frowned. "It's exposure for me and good for you."

Alondra smiled. "Remember you said that."

Sage blinked before recognizing the nervous lip bite. "What are you not telling me?"

"Troy is the photographer."

Sage opened her mouth to talk but closed it before throwing her right hand up to wave the bartender over. "I need another drink please!"

Sage and Troy were together for two and a half years. He was the best boyfriend; very supportive and romantic. He was even there to help Sage through her brother's death and her parent's divorce. All of his amazing qualities were voided when he broke Sage's heart. She had been so blind sighted by his betrayal that she still hadn't recovered from it.

Her emotions always went to hell when she thought of Troy because they usually shifted to Demetrius when that happened. Troy and Demetrius had been associates and that was how Sage met Troy in the first place. Demetrius hated the idea of them dating, but learned to accept it once they'd gotten serious. He'd often joke that Sage only wanted to date Troy because she knew he was against it. Although that was partially true, Sage stuck around because of Troy's attentiveness to her.

He cheated on her before Demetrius died. She was content with staying with him for some odd reason. He'd seemed to be holding up his promise to not cheat again. Even when Demetrius died, Troy was a big comfort. Sage just fell out of love. It wasn't until after her brother was killed that Sage realized life was too short to deal with things like infidelity. The trust was gone and soon after, so was the love.

She wasn't too excited to see him, but she knew she had to push her emotions to the side. Nowadays, Sage was all about her business and this was an opportunity to reach more clients. Troy being the photographer would not come in the way of that.

A couple of weeks later, Sage sat on her couch as Alondra read the interview on Tiffany's website.

"These pictures look really good," Alondra said. "You need to use them for promo."

"Troy actually sent them to me," Sage said, looking for something to watch on Netflix. She could feel Alondra staring at her. "It's not that deep, sis."

"What did the email say?" she asked, ignoring her sister's obvious plea not to discuss her ex.

"Nothing. It literally was just a link to the site to download the pictures."

"He so weak for that."

"Among other things," Sage said. "You know Mommy called me again about coming to visit for D's birthday."

Alondra fell back on the couch and sighed. "After last year's disaster?"

"She said Daddy not invited."

"How is she not going to invite Daddy? Like he needs an invite to celebrate his son's birthday?"

"He ain't really seem too invested in being there last year anyway."

Alondra sucked her teeth. "Okay. We are not doing this today. We've been good lately."

"I'm not trying to do anything, Londra. I'm just telling you what Mommy said. I'm going. Haven't decided if I'm driving or flying. You do what you want."

Alondra didn't respond so Sage left it alone. Although they technically avoided an argument, Sage could feel the energy shift. She sighed, pulling her phone from under her thigh to

7

check her emails. She smiled when she saw she had a new consultation request.

"Have you heard of Harris Trucking and Construction?" Sage asked. Alondra frowned and shook her head.

"What about them?"

"Nothing…"

Sage googled the company and ended up on their website. It wasn't much so she wondered what they would need from her. Doing her due diligence, she responded to the email with her pre-written script that laid out her information and how to schedule a consultation. She'd gotten so caught up in work that she hadn't really been paying attention to Alondra.

"What did you say, Lon?"

She sighed. "Sage, when is the last time you even spoke to Daddy?"

"A few weeks ago," Sage said, absentmindedly.

"Really? What did y'all talk about?"

"I told him, happy birthday."

Alondra sucked her teeth. "Sage! His birthday was like five weeks ago."

She frowned. "I said a few."

Alondra shook her head, but the look Sage gave her advised her to leave the topic alone.

"Anyway, I'm about to head out. Chris is taking me out."

Sage smirked at the mention of her sister's boyfriend. "Where to? He's paying right?"

Alondra sucked her teeth. "I tell you I paid for one date and now you're acting like I'm a sugar momma or something."

"I just don't want him to get comfortable with that."

"I don't have a problem taking my man on dates," Alondra said. "You should try it."

Sage knew that she was teasing her, but she took the dig to heart. Waving her sister off, she went back to looking at the website for Harris Trucking and Construction. She ended up on their Facebook page, which wasn't much except for some reviews from clients.

"Well, at least they have that," Sage thought as she continued her deep dive. She hadn't even noticed that Alondra left without saying anything else.

Two

Pierre Harris strolled into the downtown building on Washington Avenue that has hosted his growing business for the better part of a year with a smile from ear to ear.

"Good morning, Mr. Harris," the building receptionist greeted as she smiled towards him. She raised her hand and Pierre noticed the note between her long, pink fingernails. "Just two messages today."

"Thank you, Jessica," he said, "You know you can just forward these to my inbox right?" he asked, heading towards the elevator.

"Call me old fashioned," she replied. "You busy for lunch?" she called after him. He smiled with his back to her.

"I'm sorry sweetheart, I am."

He heard her suck her teeth before the elevator door closed. He thought it was funny how Jessica kept saying she was old fashioned but insisted on asking him out every chance she got. Pierre slid his personal phone from his pocket and checked a few messages before putting it on do not disturb. The ding alerted him that he had arrived on the 7th floor, so he stepped off the elevator. Rounding the corner, he smiled at the name on the wall.

Harris Trucking and Construction.

He quickly unlocked the door and went over to the alarm system, typing his passcode in to stop the loud beeping that filled the room. A click of the switch near him filled the office with light and warmth that he appreciated before taking his pea coat off and hanging it in the closet.

The space he rented held two offices, a conference room, a small break room, and a waiting area near the elevator. Although it wasn't too much, his company was growing due to being able to independently contract a lot of things. Pierre had bought his first diesel truck on his own a few years ago after he got his CDL. He bought it used and had so many issues with it within the first year that he decided to find some investors to purchase his next truck brand new. It was two years ago when he was able to stop driving, put another driver in his truck and hire his cousin, Julian, to run the construction part of the business. He ran a small team that he contracted out for jobs.

"Why is he always late?" Pierre mumbled to himself as he pulled his cell phone out to call Julian. Just as he was pressing send, he heard him getting off the elevator. "Julian! For real?"

"Calm down," Julian, said, strolling around the corner. "The meeting isn't for 20 more minutes and I got breakfast."

Pierre's nose flared. "That's your problem. You always worried about food."

"Nah, that's your problem. If you feed these people they wouldn't be so mad at you all the time," Julian joked.

"...How are you gonna feed 7 people with one bag from Bread Co?"

Julian smiled. "This mine. Nicole bringing the rest up."

Nicole was their assistant. Although they were doing well, they didn't have a budget for each of them to have their own, but luckily Nicole handled anything that the office needed handled. However, like Jessica, Nicole was also a big flirt. Deciding he didn't want to deal with Nicole's flirting, Pierre patted his cousin on his shoulder. "Have fun with that. I'll be in my office prepping."

Pierre shut his office door and sighed, already feeling the tension in his shoulders. Julian thought everything was a joke and never took anything serious. How could Pierre even remotely relax with his shareholders breathing down his neck every second they could?

Harris Trucking and Construction had four investors, including Jaren Harris, Pierre's father. Jaren wanted his only son to be a lawyer. When Pierre got his CDL, Jaren was disappointed and didn't mind telling him. It wasn't until Pierre paid off his first truck and made a profit that he finally accepted his son's career choice. Pierre wasn't sold on allowing his father and three other businessmen to buy into his brand, but it had been working thus far.

About six months ago, Julian noticed that the increase in their profit was slowing down and they couldn't figure out why. They were consistently booking loads with reputable companies and the construction team worked well during the seasons when weather allowed. Pierre figured the issue was somewhere in their expenses and he would figure it out soon. Jaren and the other shareholders were getting impatient. They had expected a higher return on their investment by now.

Julian stuck his head inside Pierre's office before knocking on the door frame.

"They're downstairs," Julian announced.

Pierre sighed as he stood up. "Let's get this over with."

Following Julian into the small conference room, Pierre sighed when his father came into view.

"Don't look so happy to see me, son," Jaren said, patting his shoulder.

"Any other day, I am," Pierre said. Jaren laughed as Pierre and Julian greeted the rest of the shareholders. Pierre nodded at Julian, who then began to pass out the packets they prepared for the meeting, along with the stub of the quarterly payout.

Since it was all directly deposited, each of them had already seen their payment. Each of them had already voiced how dissatisfied they were.

"Son....Mr. Harris," Jaren said, correcting himself. "You know based on your own calculations, our return on investment should be solely profit by now."

"Mr. Harris," Julian tried to interject as he and Pierre had planned. "We know we are a little behind schedule as far as payout, but we have consist…"

Jaren held his hand up. "With all due respect, we know how to read and we can comprehend what is going on. I'd like the other Mr. Harris in the room to explain what he's going to do about it."

Pierre smiled. "We are more than capable of meeting the demands of the industry and keeping you all in the loop with your investments. However, we have taken the initiative to hire a consultant who works with small businesses such as Harris Trucking and Construction in order to push us to the next level. Once the evaluation is done, we can make strides to make sure your quarterly checks grow."

"And when does this consultant start?"

Three

It had been Julian's idea to hire a consultant. When he first brought the idea to Pierre, he figured it would just be some new age entrepreneur who wanted to change their logo and give their social media pages an uplift. Pierre didn't think that this consultant could do anything tangible to increase their bottom line. When Julian explained to him what the service actually was, Pierre was upset. Changing the image of the brand was one thing, but digging into their logistics, procedures, and financials was a whole other ball game. There weren't too many people Pierre trusted with that and it surely wasn't a woman he'd never met.

"How do you know this chick is credible?" Pierre asked.

"I told you I found her on this blog's site that interviewed her. She has a lot of reviews. Seems legit."

"I don't even want to do this," Pierre groaned.

"Why do I always have to hold your hand through every meeting," Julian teased. "You childish."

Pierre couldn't help but laugh. "Why are you so comfortable with asking someone outside of our business for help anyway?"

"It ain't even like that," Julian said. "I just know it'll keep Uncle Jay and the old heads off of us for a little bit.

Sometimes you have to play the game, cuz. And look, if she actually finds something we haven't been able to see then it's a win-win."

Pierre sat back in his leather chair and ran his hand down his face. "I guess."

"No time for guessing," Julian stated, standing up. "Meeting's in 10."

"I need a vacation after this," Pierre mumbled to himself. Julian heard him and chuckled.

"You don't even work that hard," he teased. "You probably couldn't even take a 300-mile load anymore."

Pierre frowned. "You're crazy. That's easy money!"

"Yeah, okay," Julian laughed. They heard the elevator ding as they walked out of Julian's office and towards the conference room. "Looks like she's right on time."

Pierre watched a short woman with caramel skin round the corner and stop at Nicole's desk. She was slim but seemed to have a little weight on her that curved in a pair of burgundy dress pants that fit snug on her hips and flared out a little. His eyes travelled up past the ruffled collar of her button up shirt, over her neck, full lips, and rounded nose. Pierre misstepped as he looked into her big, dark brown eyes. They shined just a little as she smiled, greeting Nicole with a firm handshake. He watched her bite the corner of her lip before laughing, both women then looking towards them.

"Oh!" Nicole said. "I didn't see you two there. I was going to escort Miss Anderson to the conference room.

"We'll take it from here," Julian said, stepping up. "Nice to meet you. I'm Julian."

"Oh you're who I spoke with on the phone," she stated. "Nice to meet you, too. I'm Sage."

"This is my partner, Pierre."

Noticing his hand wasn't out to shake hers, Sage gripped her bag and nodded. "Hello."

"How are you?" he asked.

"I'm good," she smiled again. "Ready to get to work."

Julian held his hand out towards the hallway. "Please, follow me."

The three went into the conference room and Pierre rolled his eyes. Julian already had pastries and other snacks on the table. Julian pointed towards an empty chair for Sage. She nodded and took a seat, immediately pulling some notebooks and a tablet out of her bag.

"I'd like to start by saying thank you for hiring me to assist your company at this time. I've read over your mission and values and I'm excited to help where I can. I also want to make a disclaimer that although I am the only consultant at Sage Consulting, I have prided myself on my commitment to take care of my clients and will not take any other clients while I am working with you. You have my experience, skill, knowledge, and undivided attention."

Julian nodded, looking at Pierre for some type of response. Pierre looked at the woman in front of him and nodded in the same manner his cousin had. However, he wasn't sold on her little speech.

"Sage is your real name?" Pierre asked. She frowned.

"Excuse me?"

"I figured it was some play on words with how you could cleanse a business," he laughed. "Wow. Sage?"

Her nostrils flared as she looked down at her screen. "Miss Anderson will do just fine."

Pierre cleared his throat. "No, Sage is a..um...nice name."

She slowly looked up at his face. "Miss Anderson will do."

He smirked. "Okay...Miss Anderson. You should know that I've hired you against my will."

She sat back in the leather chair, her turn to smirk. "I'm actually not surprised. Silent partner? Shareholders?"

"Shareholders," he confirmed.

Sage's face lit up with recognition as she nodded. "Uh hum. Well, let's not waste anymore time with pleasantries. This is a list of the files I'll need access to in order to conduct my evaluation. I'll also need to conduct interviews and shadowing of all of your employees, starting with any supervisors and managers who have direct reporting employees."

"Can you explain your process?"

"I go over everything given and your brand as it looks from the outside looking in. Once I have enough information I can perform a SWOT analysis and provide specific recommendations on how to increase your bottom line, make your shareholders happy, increase your brand recognition, and ultimately increase your profit. My reports will include this information as well as steps to implement if you chose to."

"If we chose to?" he asked, raising an eyebrow. Sage placed her hands flat on her tablet, looked up at him and smiled.

"Of course," she replied. "This is your company. I just provide suggestions based on my expertise."

He slowly nodded. "Do you have credentials? Reviews? Proven statistics?"

"Links to all of the above are on my website. Would you like me to pull it up for you?" she asked, pointing at the large monitor on the wall. Pierre waved his hand.

"That won't be necessary."

"I've read them," Julian said, finally stepping in. "I'm excited to see what you discover."

Pierre read over the list Sage handed him while she and Julian made small talk. "There's no way I'm giving you access to all of this. How is this relevant to my company moving forward?"

"Did you read my contract?" Sage asked, trying not to roll her eyes.

"Of course I did," he said.

"Well, then you are aware of my 21-day progession guarantee. I have clearly stated all confidentiality and discretion will be used and none of your information will be leaked. You agreed to that. In order for me to do my job, I'll need your cooperation."

He sighed. "I can bend on some things, but…"

"Mr. Harris, there are no buts. I'll need these requested items by Wednesday in order to begin next Monday. If you'd like to terminate our contract, there is a clause in my contract that states all fees that are associated with that," Sage, closed her laptop and slid it into its bag so smoothly, it didn't register to Pierre she was leaving. "I'll be in my office until 4p today. You can contact me with any questions. Have a nice day."

Pierre blinked. His conference room had never been this quiet as he kept his eyes trained on the door, halfheartedly waiting for Sage to walk back in and apologize.

Julian began to chuckle and Pierre threw a pen at him. "Shut up." Julian raised both hands in surrender, but did not give up his smile.

Four

"Then this man had the nerve...the nerve...to ask if Sage was my real name!"

"Oh Lord," Sage's best friend, Carmen, said as she poured more wine into Sage's glass. "And he's still breathing?"

Alondra laughed. "Now C, you know this is the new and improved Sage we're talking to. Not old Sage. Old Sage would have been telling us this story on the way from county."

Sage rolled her eyes as they both laughed. "Can I finish my story, please?"

"Hold on," Alondra said, holding her glass towards Carmen. "Refill please."

Sage smirked, shaking her head at them before taking a sip from her own glass. "He's hell bent on not being cooperative. I emailed him and his partner, cousin or whatever he is, after our meeting and he still wanted to tell me he wasn't happy about giving me access to all his information. He started this company but his shareholders seem to be pressuring him."

"Hell, I would be too," Carmen said. "They want those quarterly checks!"

Sage nodded and turned back towards the stove to check her alfredo sauce. She had a long day but was glad to catch up with her favorite people while cooking them a meal. It was

Alondra's turn to pick the meal and Sage was happy she'd chosen an easy dish; seafood alfredo.

Sage and Carmen met in college. Sage had requested a dorm transfer at SIUE because of her roommate's creepy boyfriend. Carmen had a double room but her roommate had dropped out the previous semester. She wasn't too happy about sharing a room again. After a few weeks of petty arguments, they bonded over old Disney shows and became friends.

"So when do you have to see Rude Bae again?" Alondra said.

"Girl what? We're labeling this man Rude Bae?" Carmen asked.

"I looked him up on Facebook," she admitted. "He's definitely a bae type."

"Oh! Let me see," Carmen said.

"Alondra!" Sage said, laughing at her sister's audacity.

"What?" she asked, innocently. "I needed a visual for this story."

Carmen looked down at Alondra's phone and smirked. Sage tried to glance at her phone without being obvious, although she could see Pierre in her head without a visual. Pierre was a little over 6 feet with a lean build but somewhat muscular. He filled out a suit well; it was the first thing Sage noticed about him. He had an amazing smile with one dimple and brown eyes that shined when he was being sarcastic. Pierre kept a low fade full of waves and his goatee was cut close to his chin.

"Oh yeah, he's Rude Bae from now on. Sage, you did not tell us he was fine!"

"That was irrelevant to my frustration."

"Is it really? Because something about a man who is fine and rude just does it for me," Alondra said. "When you finally get him you know he's not Mr. Friendly to every girl up in his face."

"I could care less about any of that."

"Just admit he can be rude and fine at the same time," Carmen egged on. Alondra giggled.

Sage shook her head. "No, he's rude," she said, trying to get them to look past Pierre's looks. Sage would be lying to herself if she hadn't noticed Pierre's attractiveness, but no one had to know that. "Hopefully he'll just email me everything and I won't have to see him until it's time to give my recommendation."

Alondra and Carmen raised their glasses. "Here's to hope."

A week later, Sage found herself back on the elevator on the way up to Harris Trucking and Construction. She smiled at Nicole as she walked up to her desk. "Good morning. I have an 8 am with Mr. Harris."

"Oh," Nicole said. "He isn't in yet, but he asked me to let you in the conference room and he should be here shortly."

Sage frowned. "What exactly is shortly? I am on a schedule and he's not being very respectful of that."

Nicole sat back in her chair and looked up at Sage. "All he said was he would be here shortly. I can let you in the conference room or you can wait in your car if you'd like."

Sage eyed her. "The conference room is fine."

Nicole smiled. "Great. Follow me."

The annoyance in Nicole's voice was not lost on Sage, but she decided to ignore it since she was there on business. She wasn't one to let things like that go unchecked. Sage paced herself, putting a little bit of space between them before following her to the conference room. Nicole pivoted when she opened the door, holding it open for Sage.

"Would you like anything?" Nicole asked with a tight smile. "Coffee?"

Sage held up her travel mug. "I'm covered. Thanks."

She walked in the door past Nicole and placed her bag on the table. Nicole closed the door behind her and Sage rolled her eyes.

"Don't have time for this," she mumbled, sitting down in the same chair she'd sat in the last time and unzipped her bag.

Sage sighed as she triple checked her documents while waiting for Pierre. She had been more prepared for his crassness this time around and made sure all of her information was on point. She had done a SWOT analysis on his brand with an emphasis on his competitors who were public. This way she could compare their financials and see if there was something obvious that Harris Trucking & Construction wasn't doing. He had given her access to most of the things she requested, but not all. Sage knew it was a test and she was more than willing to prove her worth as a consultant.

Once she was satisfied with her prep, Sage pulled out her phone to see it was 8:10a. She rolled her eyes, pulling up both Julian and Pierre's number to send them a group text asking if they needed to reschedule. Just as she hit send, she heard a voice outside of the conference room. The bravado tone asked Nicole for a cup of coffee and she giddily agreed. Sage rolled her eyes again.

"Lord, get me through."

The conference door opened and Pierre walked in solo. He was looking down at his phone as he unbuttoned his suit jacket. When he finally looked up at Sage he smiled.

"Apologies for being late," he said, holding up his phone to show her message. "It'll just be you and me today. Julian had a prior engagement." Sage felt her face get hot as she sat up straight, pushing her back from the chair. Pierre watched her as he rounded the table.

"If you needed to reschedule, you could have done so."

"I'm here," Pierre said, sitting down.

"15 minutes late."

"I just apologized for that," he said. "Don't make a big deal out of 15 minutes. You can still leave at 9."

"I plan to," Sage said. "You don't seem to be cooperating anyway."

Pierre sat back in the leather chair and sighed, rubbing his forehead with his fingertips. "What are you talking about now?"

"You haven't released all the required information I need," Sage said. "You know that, but seem to think I wouldn't notice. However, I have another solution that you may find more suitable."

Pierre's right eyebrow raised. "And what's that?"

"Access to your managers and anyone in a supervisory role. I can conduct interviews with them and shadow them in their daily duties to get the information I need."

He sighed. "So you want me to tell grown men they have a babysitter?"

"I don't need you to tell them anything. Just give me their schedules and tell them to expect to indulge me for a few hours of their day. No harm."

"You know this is day 7 of your supposed 21-day guarantee right?"

"Which is exactly why I'll need those schedules at the end of the day," Sage said, she pushed her tablet towards him. "Now, here's what I've gathered so far. I want you to double check to make sure it's accurate before I move forward."

The noticeable change in Pierre's posture made Sage sit up straight. She could tell a little of his defense fell since she hadn't bought into his antagonizing comments and she inwardly smiled.

"I guess that's not so bad," he relented with relaxed shoulders. "You don't mind going to construction sites do you? I'll make sure it's a safe area."

Sage nodded. "I'd appreciate that, thank you."

"I'm a gentleman before anything," he said, lightly. Sage smirked.

"I hadn't noticed," she teased. Pierre looked up at her in confusion, but smirked when he saw her facial expression. He pointed his finger at her and smiled.

"You're something else, Ms. Anderson."

"...Sage is fine."

Five

Within the next week, Sage and Pierre's working relationship became a little less hostile. Spending time with his employees had given Sage insight on the business as well as Pierre himself. Sage had learned that Pierre was quite popular. He was a member of Kappa Alpha Psi, which she could have guessed. Pierre had an air about him that teetered between confidence and arrogance. He was a pretty boy, for sure. His employees seemed to enjoy working for him as well. Besides the normal working complaints, everyone seemed to be happy at the company and that made her excited to help them grow. However, it also became a stressor for Sage. Even after collecting all of the data and interviews, she wasn't really sure why they weren't progressing as they should be.

Since their operations seemed to run smoothly, Sage began to take a look at their marketing strategy. Maybe if she could help them target a more exclusive clientele, she could help them create more connections with major companies. Since Pierre handled the marketing, that meant they would spend more time together.

On that particular day, Sage and Pierre were in his office on the black, plush couch in front of his coffee table. Sage had kicked off her shoes and folded her legs under her body as she sat with her back against the arm of the couch, typing away on her iPad. Since it was Friday, she was dressed casually in a pair of jeans and an oversized sweater. On the other end of the couch, Pierre watched her discreetly.

He noticed her beauty whenever she was quiet. Her short frame was naturally curvy but Pierre could tell that she didn't flaunt it often. He looked at her full lips and found himself wanting to hear her voice.

"Did you eat yet? I might order in for lunch."

"I'm good," Sage said. Pierre noted the calm in her tone and chuckled. "What?"

"You went from being defensive in my conference room to real comfortable on my couch," he said. Sage's eyes grew wide.

"Oh, I'm sorry," she said, attempting to unfold her legs.

"No," he said, holding his hand out to stop her. "I don't mind. Just making an observation."

Sage blushed. "I have to get comfortable when I'm brainstorming. What made you choose your particular target market?"

"Accessibility," he said without hesitation. Sage waited to see if he would say more.

"...That's it?"

"It's the truth," he shrugged.

"Okay. What would your ideal client look like?" she asked.

Pierre sat back, stretching his arm along the back of the couch as he looked up at the ceiling. Sage giggled at his serious face.

"Amazon or Walmart."

"What?"

"I know they have their own trucks and everything, but contracts with them are my ideal client."

"So major corporations who haul necessities?"

Pierre glanced at Sage and smirked. "Yeah, I guess that sums it up." She nodded before typing back on her iPad. "Why do you ask?"

"Trying to build a profile of your ideal client so we can brainstorm some marketing strategies."

Pierre groaned. "Our marketing is fine. I don't need all that fluff and social media mess. We get contracts fine."

"You want your shareholders to be satisfied right?"

"Of course."

"And increasing your profit would do so. Now, I know you don't want to just work harder. You have to work smarter. Bringing in your ideal clientele brings in your ideal profit. It's a win-win for everyone."

Pierre scratched the top of his head before relaxing his shoulders. Sage smirked, but did not respond. She knew he could tell her statement made sense. She wouldn't rub it in. Instead, she handed him her iPad so he could see the notes that she had so far."Anyone ever told you that you'd be a good lawyer?" he asked. Sage frowned.

"No."

"Well...you would."

"I'm not sure if that's an insult or a compliment," Sage laughed. Pierre just shrugged and kept reading over her notes. Sage shook her head before stretching the sleeves of her sweater over her hands.

"How many interviews do you have left?" he asked.

"Let me see," she said, holding her hand out for her iPad. Pierre gave it back before standing up to walk over to the mini fridge in the corner of his office. "I have 3 left. Your operations manager, the HR specialist, and Julian."

"Save him for last," Pierre joked. Sage laughed.

"What's the story on you two?" she asked. "You're always fighting."

"Not really fighting. Just cousin behavior."

Sage smiled, thinking of Alondra. "You act like brothers."

"Grew up that way."

"Are you an only child?"

Pierre pulled a bottle of water out, holding it towards Sage. She shook her head. "I am. Can't you tell?"

"Now that you mentioned it..." Pierre frowned and Sage laughed. "I'm playing. Well, not really but you get what I mean."

"I don't," he said, rolling his eyes. Sage found his fake outrage to be funny.

"Don't be so sensitive," she said. "You have only child tendencies that's all."

"Okay...just like you have the oldest child tendencies."

Sage shrugged. "It's possible."

"I bet you get on your sister's nerves."

Sage sighed, suddenly thinking about the rocky state of her and Alondra's relationship in previous years. It was steady now, but after her brother's death and their parents divorce, there was a change between them. Alondra sided with their dad for reasons Sage would never understand. They clashed a lot. Alondra always said Sage had to be right. Alondra was hard headed and content on learning everything herself instead of learning from her sister's mistakes. What good was Sage if she couldn't help her sister in life by making her falls a little less painful? Sage did push Alondra in certain areas of her life, but that was what all big sisters did, wasn't it?

"She probably can't even stand you," Pierre said. That line snapped Sage out of her own thoughts.

"You might want to quit while you're ahead."

Pierre noticed the change in her tone again and sighed as he reclaimed his seat on the couch. "Back to business then."

Sage sighed before nodding. "No, actually time's up."

"We went over everything?" Pierre asked.

"For now," she lied. "Don't you have another meeting soon?"

Pierre looked at his watch and stood up quickly. "You're right. I'm actually running behind."

Sage smirked. "*Figures*," she thought. It was just as well since Sage had decided it was time for her to leave. She didn't like how personal their conversation had gotten.

"You mind if I head out? Julian should be here soon and Nicole's still out front."

"Yeah, go ahead. I'll schedule our next meeting with her."

"Actually, I have something else in mind," Pierre said with a smirk. Sage looked on in confusion. "Don't worry. You'll like it. Keep an eye on your inbox."

Before she could protest, Pierre left her in his office. She sat there for a moment, looking around at her things scattered on the coffee table and his wall-mounted television that played KMOV news on mute.

"He's crazy," she said, sitting up to pack her things up. She slipped her boots back on and headed out of his office. She ran into Julian on her way out. "Hey. How was your meeting?"

Julian smiled. "Hello, Ms. Anderson. The better question is did you and my cousin make it through today without scratching each other's eyes out?"

Sage laughed. "We weren't that bad."

Julian chuckled. "I'm happy you two are getting along."

"Speaking of," Sage said. "He mentioned something about an event invitation coming to my inbox? You know what that is?"

Julian smiled. "He didn't tell you which means I won't either," he said. "Have a good day!"

Sage huffed as he walked off towards his office. "Fine then!" she called after him. He laughed and waved in the air. Sage had to laugh at that herself before leaving out of their office space and getting on the elevator.

Six

Pierre invited Sage to an auction that weekend. He said he was interested in purchasing at least one truck and another trailer and thought Sage may like to see the process. She was very interested, but her brother's birthday was that weekend and she promised to drive home with Alondra to spend it with their mother and grandmother.

The night before the two were set to get on the highway, Sage was on the phone with their mother, Kara.

"Someone said, 'mother of two grown girls where?'" Sage said, reading the comments on her latest appreciation post.

"Oh, I like his energy," Kara said. Sage giggled.

"You better not like no young man's energy, woman."

"I may not look like it, but don't forget I'm your momma."

Sage smiled. "I miss you. Can't wait to see you and Granny."

"I can't tell," Kara said. "It takes your forever to come home."

"You know I'd be there more often if I could," Sage said. "And you didn't have to move."

"Yes, I did."

Sage left that comment alone. "Are we doing anything special?"

Kara sighed. "I'm not sure. Thought about a balloon release."

"Kind of cliche, Mommy."

"That's what Lonny said!"

"And he hated balloons."

"That's what your granny said."

Sage giggled, that warm feeling of memories of her little brother flooded her mind. "He stayed popping mine anytime I got them. Especially Valentine's Day."

"My big protective baby," Kara said. "I can't believe this will be his sixth birthday without him." Even though she knew her mother couldn't see her, Sage nodded.

"Okay, let me hit these sheets so we can get on the road early."

"Be safe and let me know when you get on the highway. Kiss my other baby for me."

"I'm not kissing her."

"I heard that!" Alondra said, coming out of Sage's bathroom. Kara laughed.

"Good night, girls."

"I saw a post where a lot of his friends are going to be up at the park they used to play ball at on Saturday," Alondra said, getting into Sage's bed on the right side.

"That's nice."

"Yeah, I would have gone if we weren't going home."

"Mommy seems less sad than last year," Sage said.

Alondra nodded, tying her satin scarf around her hair that was up in a pineapple; her curls on top of her head. "You're driving first."

"I know that," Sage said, getting comfortable in her spot. "Good night."

Highway 64 East was sprinkled with cars before 5am. Although she hadn't had a full 8 hours of sleep, Sage was excited about seeing her mom and grandmother, so she perked up to take the first shift driving. She had a pre-made road trip playlist, her iced coffee, and a few bags of Chex mix. Alondra, on the other hand, was still in sleep mode. She was already in the passenger seat of their rental car with her shoes off, wrapped in a blanket.

"So you won't be much company huh?" Sage said.

"Sorry, sis."

Sage laughed before waving her off. "You good because I'll definitely be sleeping when it's your turn."

"Exactly," Alondra said, reclining the seat back. "Goodnight."

Sage laughed before turning the music up a little. She found a nice speed and put it on cruise control before taking a sip of her coffee. While she drove, Sage thought about her business and how she could move to the next level. She wondered if she could budget for an assistant so she could be free to do a little more. Being around Pierre and Julian had opened her eyes to a few business practices that she wanted to implement. It was hard being in business, especially by yourself. However, Sage was nervous about employing others. Would she be dependable enough to provide someone else with a steady paycheck?

Sage frowned when she heard "Sumthin' Sumthin'" by Maxwell play again. Her playlist was pretty long, but she was sure she'd heard this one at least twice before seeing that she had been driving for over five hours. Alondra had been up after their last pit stop, typing away on her phone.

"Londra, you have to drive now," Sage said, pressing her hand into the steering wheel. "You've been up for an hour."

Alondra chuckled as she put her phone down. "Well, you looked like you were having fun."

Sage rolled her eyes, looking for the best exit to get off on. "You're so spoiled."

"Your fault."

Sage found an exit for a QuikTrip and decided to fill the tank up and get more snacks. When she got back to the car, Alondra was in the driver's seat with her phone hooked up to the bluetooth. Sage laughed.

"You couldn't wait."

"Come on, boo!" Alondra said. "We gotta be on the I-10 by 10!"

They both laughed as Alondra quoted *Johnson Family Vacation*. Sage got in the passenger seat and got comfortable as Alondra pulled out of the gas station. She frowned as loud bass came through the speakers.

"Oh Lord," she said.

"Don't do that, I listened to your old school playlist," Alondra said.

"It wasn't all old school!" Sage said, trying not to laugh. Alondra smirked but didn't respond. Sage pulled out her phone and went to her Instagram app, taking a picture of Alondra in the driver's seat. She used the Poll Option to ask her followers for playlist suggestions since her sister was a trap queen. "You can handle the last 4 hours?"

Alondra nodded. "Yes, try to stay up though. I know you'll be asleep in a hot second."

Sage chuckled. "I'll do what I can."

Her phone buzzed and she was surprised to see Pierre had responded to her poll. They followed each other last week during their meeting but hadn't interacted on social media up until then. She was shocked to see he told her to listen to Sir's new album. She decided to respond to him with a post she made a few days ago listening to "Hair Down." When she shared his answer on her story, she put the caption, "Already a fav, sir."

He responded in her direct messages: **You're gorgeous when you aren't coming for my head.**

Sage felt her skin heat up and she immediately chastised herself. She looked to see if her sister was paying her any attention and relaxed in her chair once she noticed Alondra was focused on the road.

"Got 4 hours left," Sage thought. *"Might as well entertain this."*

Sage sent Pierre a message back, challenging him to put a playlist together that he thought fit her. She was anxious to see what he sent her. They'd bumped heads on more than one occasion and Sage knew for sure that he assumed some things about her that were not true. She was ready to chew his head off if he sent something inappropriate.

She raised one eyebrow when he challenged her back. Saying they'd go round for round and see who came out on top. Sage smirked before sending him a thumbs up, telling him to go first.

The first song he sent her was "On to the Next One" by Jay-Z saying that he was sure she listened to this before all of her meetings. Sage laughed, causing Alondra to look at her.

"What are you laughing at?"

Sage smirked before shaking her head. "Something on IG, you know the internet has no chill," she lied.

Alondra chuckled. "Tell me about it." She went back to rapping along with whatever she was listening to as Sage thought about what to send as her first track for Pierre. She double tapped her home screen and pulled up her playlist and scrolled a little. She sent "Wipe me Down" and said, "Because all you Kappas are the same."

Pierre sent a laughing emoji back. **Good one.**

They went back and forth with each other. Sage was pleasantly surprised at how many songs Pierre picked for her that she had recently played. He threw a few songs in there that she absolutely hated, but even then it was a joke about how he knew she wouldn't like it.

Music was a big deal to Sage. It was literally a form of therapy and she found herself slightly bothered that he had made her so well. They weren't friends and hardly liked working with each other. She was shocked that she had guessed some of his favorite tracks, too. How were they able to know each other's music selections so well?

"Okay, who are you caking with?"

Sage looked up to see Alondra looking from the road to her. She sighed when she noticed familiar signs that told her they were finally in North Carolina. "Dang, we're almost home?"

"Sure are, Captain Obvious, now get back to the question at hand."

Sage sighed. "You know Pierre Harris that I told you about?"

"Rude Bae that's been cussing you out at work?" Alondra said with a smirk. Sage rolled her eyes.

"Yeah okay," she said. "Anyway. I asked for songs on IG and we got into this battle of who can guess each other's favorite music."

"That's real corny, sis," Alondra said. "Cute, but corny."

Sage pouted. "And he's legit on here guessing my life away."

Alondra laughed. "He's old school like you?"

"Shut up and get me to my grandma," Sage said. Alondra laughed.

Sage and Alondra's grandmother, Madie, was from Charlotte but had moved to the St. Louis area when she met their grandpa. It wasn't until after Alondra graduated high school and their grandpa passed away that she moved back to Charlotte to be closer to her brothers and sister. About a year after their brother's death, their mom moved back as well.

"Mommy is blowing my phone up like she has GPS on us," Alondra said, getting off the highway to get to their parent's house.

"She probably does," Sage said, deciding to call her on speakerphone. "Hey Mommy. We're pulling up."

"Good because I'm hungry and your granny won't let me eat!"

"Dang," Alondra said. "So you just didn't miss your daughters huh?"

"I'll miss y'all after we eat."

Sage and Alondra laughed. She was about to tell her to open the door as the house came in sight, but she was already standing on the porch.

Kara was your typical black mother. She was in her late 50's but didn't look a day over 30. Ever since she'd taken her health seriously, she was looking younger by the day. Alondra looked more like Kara than Sage did, but you could tell that she was their mother. Demetrius, on the other hand, looked like Kara's twin.

"About time my sugar dolls got here," she said, holding both her arms out. Sage and Alondra playfully groaned, but walked into their mother's open arms anyway. They both giggled as she rocked them side to side, kissing them both on the cheek. Their union was cut short as the screen door swung open.

"You were so hungry two minutes ago, now you're acting like you haven't seen them in a month of Sundays."

Sage smiled, being the first to break the hug to greet her favorite person. "Hey Granny."

"Hi baby," she said, pulling Sage into a hug. "Get on in there and wash up to eat."

"Yes ma'am," Sage said, walking into the house as Madie greeted Alondra. Her heart melted at the familiar aromas filling the air. She could smell the cinnamon candles her grandmother loved to burn, but they were not overwhelmed by the smell of her aromatic spices. Sage picked up her pace to get to the downstairs bathroom to wash her hands.

"Fried cabbage, mac and cheese, hot water cornbread and catfish," Madie said. "Welcome home."

"Oh please pray so I can eat!" Alondra said. Madie swatted her arm and she laughed.

"Lord, thank you for bringing our girls home safely. We ask that you bless this food we are about to receive. Let it go to the nourishment of our bodies and let these flavors float all the way up there to my grandson who loved his Granny's fried cabbage. Amen."

"Amen!"

"So what's the plan?" Sage asked after fixing her plate.

"Well, since y'all been on the road all day, I figured we'd chill tonight and go to the cemetery tomorrow morning."

Sage nodded. Although Demetrius was killed in St. Louis, he was buried on the plot their grandfather bought when they were younger.

"The florist…"

"Already ordered," Madie said, cutting Sage off. Alondra smiled as she stuffed her mouth with cabbage. Sage's phone buzzed on the table and just as she reached for it, Kara tapped her hand.

"You know we don't do phones at the table."

"Sorry," Sage said, sliding it into her pocket. Kara smiled before placing her palm against Sage's cheek before turning to pull one of Alondra's curls.

"I'm glad my babies are home."

"Me too," Sage and Alondra said, simultaneously.

"Save some room for this dessert I'm making," Madie said.

"Oh, I can't wait to eat that," Sage said, smelling the cake in the oven. "Haven't had one in so long."

"Red velvet was Demetrius' favorite," Kara said.

As always when the late Demetrius was brought up, the room fell into a nostalgic silence. It wasn't always a comfortable one, but time made it hurt just a little less.

"So," she said. "When is the last time you've spoken to Donovan Anderson?"

Alondra smiled while Sage tried not to roll her eyes.

"I spoke to Daddy before we got on the road," she said, eyeing her big sister. "We talk a lot."

"That's good," Kara said. "I'm glad to hear that."

"But I don't know about Sage."

"Really, Londra?" Sage asked. "Had to go there huh?"

"Mommy asked!"

"Quit it," Kara said, before looking at her oldest. "He doesn't call you?"

"He does," Sage said. "I'm just...busy a lot. We talk though."

Kara looked at her for a moment before moving to walk away. "Okay."

"Now you're telling stories to Mommy," Alondra whispered.

"Telling stories to Mommy," Sage mocked her. "Shut up."

Later that evening after Madie went to bed, Sage, Alondra, and Kara were in her king-sized bed watching Bad Boys. Sage was going through hairstyles on Pinterest, looking for something different.

"I think I like the finger wave look," she said. "I'd have to cut my hair more."

"Oh and dye it a lighter color," Alondra said. Sage frowned. "You think?"

"Stop cutting your hair," Kara said. "I like when you had that little bob."

"That was cute."

Sage nodded, not sold on anything at the moment as she remembered the notification she got during dinner. She went

41

to her Instagram and saw a message request. She rolled her eyes to see it was from Troy.

I know D's birthday is tomorrow. Just wanted to see how everyone was.

Sage didn't respond, grateful that she didn't have to open it to read what he said. Closing the app and putting her phone on the nightstand, Sage focused on spending time with her mom and sister.

"I can't believe my little baby is finally 16!" Sage teased Demetrius, pulling on one of his locs. He sucked his teeth before pushing her hand away.

"I don't want to hear all that. You letting me get the car tonight?" he asked, smiling. Sage frowned.

"In what world do you think I'd get away with giving you my car and you don't have a license? Mommy and Daddy would kill me."

"Man," he said. "I thought you'd be less of a lame when you turned 18."

Sage laughed, even though he was trying to clown her. "I guess my lame self will keep this birthday gift then."

"I'm playing sis, I love you."

"Um hum," Sage chuckled, handing him a bag. It was small, but heavy and the jeweler's name on the bag made Demetrius grin.

"I already know this is my grill!" he said. "How you get it made without me?"

Sage sucked her teeth at the fact that he guessed correctly. "Alondra stole your retainer."

"Thief!" he said, turning to push 14-year-old Alondra on the shoulder. She kicked his thigh.

"Leave me alone. I'm over here minding my business."

"Shut up," Demetrius said, unwrapping his grill before pushing it in his mouth. "I'm about to get all the girls with this."

"You wish!" Sage and Alondra both said before laughing.

After a great night, Sage woke up the next morning in a somber mood. Holidays and birthdays always brought dreams of Demetrius. Sage loved and hated it all the same. She'd woken up just as the sun was rising; it rained during the night. Dew was on the window sills as she tiptoed to the kitchen to make a pot of coffee. She smiled to see Madie already there.

"I beat you," Madie said. Sage giggled.

"Good morning, Granny," Sage said. "You make coffee?"

"Was about to," she said. "Go ahead."

Sage nodded, noticing the open Bible sitting in front of her grandmother at the table. "I'm sorry if I interrupted."

Madie smiled. "I was just reading a few verses."

"Do you do that every morning?"

"Yes. I suggest you do the same. It'll help center you for the day."

Sage nodded, walking over to the cabinet where she knew the coffee would be. "Yes, ma'am."

"Oh! I can send you some Youtube videos of a few preachers I like."

Sage smirked. "Granny, what are you doing on Youtube?"

"I just told you," she said, side eyeing her granddaughter. Sage held her laugh in.

"I'd like that."

They heard Alondra and Kara coming down the hall, both already dressed.

"Told you," Kara said. "No matter how early I wake up, she always beats me."

"I'm your mother," Granny said. "I'm supposed to."

"So are we having breakfast first, or…" Alondra asked. Kara sighed, looking around the room.

"I think I want to visit my son before I do anything else."

Sage nodded. "I'll go get ready."

They were all dressed and ready within the hour. Sage drove the rental to the florist Madie always used before they headed to the cemetery which wasn't far from the house.

The sun was peeking out of the clouds and the wind picked up a little. Sage zipped her jacket up as Alondra led the way to the Coleson plot. There were only 4 tombstones there. Demetrius, their grandfather, and his parents.

"Don't they have people who are supposed to clean these?" Alondra asked, getting down on her knees and pulling weeds up from around Demetrius' grave. Kara pulled the dead flowers from the holder and replaced them with the fresh ones. She turned to do the same to her father's grave.

"Hey Daddy," she said. "I hope you threw a party up there for my baby's birthday."

Madie laughed. "Who threw a party? You know that man did nothing but show up to functions and eat."

They laughed.

"Don't talk about my grandpa like that," Sage said, she sat down next to Alondra, leaning her shoulder against the headstone. "Happy birthday, baby."

The cold hard ground under her made her shift before she brushed her hand over his name. Kara sat down on the opposite side while Madie leaned against her husband's headstone. Kara prayed before she began talking to her son as if no one else was there. Everyone else grew quiet, yet Sage was the first one to cry.

Her face felt hot as she fanned her hands around it, looking up at the sky to try and stop the tears before they came. She hiccuped when her heart felt heavier, Demetrius' smiling face flashing in her mind like a movie trailer. Remembering the last time she saw him alive broke her.

"It's not fair," she mumbled, wiping her face. "He wasn't even doing anything. I can't get over it. Like he wasn't doing anything." Her nose tingled as her eyes filled with more tears. "Why did it have to be him?"

Alondra interlaced their fingers as she moved closer to her. Although she was also crying, she tried to console her big sister by rubbing her back. "It's not fair."

Sage shook her head. "I just want him back. I want our family back like it was."

Kara sighed. "That's not how it works, love."

"All we can do is deal with what we've been given," Madie said. "We might be bent, but we aren't broken. This," she said, moving her hand around their circle. "Is our family. We're all we got."

After another moment of silence, Alondra leaned over Sage to get closer to the headstone. "D, Sage down here crying like usual."

Sage laughed before pushing Alondra. "Shut up."

"He always said you were a cry baby," she teased.

Sage rolled her eyes. "He cried more than the both of us."

"Now that's the truth," Kara and Madie said.

"Remember when he found out you told Amber that he slept in the bed with you because he was scared of thunderstorms?" Alondra said. Sage laughed hard, wiping the remaining tears from her face.

"I thought he was going to run me over that day," Sage said. "She cancelled their date and everything. I had to finally tell that girl I made it up."

"Knowing good and well he did it!" Alondra said. They all laughed. After spending a little more time reminiscing on times when both Demetrius and Grandpa were alive, they all decided to head home.

That night, Sage got another message from Pierre. She smiled to see it was more songs. One song in particular caught her eye because she had never heard of it. Going to her Apple

Music, Sage searched for "Gimme the Wheel" by Alina Baraz and Smino. She made it halfway through before she clicked back on her Instagram app.

SageItOut: This one by Alina is nice. Doesn't seem like something you'd listen to.

HarrisTrucks: I'm a Smino fan.

SageItOut: Oh LOL. Well either way, thank you. I'm going to listen to the rest of this album to put myself to sleep.

HarrisTrucks: Did you enjoy your time at home?

SageItOut: I did...ready to get back to work though.

HarrisTrucks: Yeah, cause I'm holding you to your guarantee.

Sage smiled, deciding not to reply. Their conversation that day had been fluid, but she wasn't surprised that he wanted to irritate her in some way. She turned her headphones down a little before getting comfortable in the guest room. Alondra was sleeping in their grandmother's bed that night.

Sage and Alondra stayed one more full day before it was time to head back to St. Louis. She smiled as she looked at the picture of her family that she posted on Instagram. Her caption read, "Breakfast before we hit the road." Sage replied to a few messages and liked a few pictures before she decided to put her phone down and finish eating. Before she did, she got a text message from Pierre.

HarrisTrucks: Let me know when you make it home.

SageItOut: Why? Our next meeting isn't until Tuesday?

HarrisTrucks: I want to take you out.

Seven

"I can't believe you're actually taking her out, bruh," Julian said, rummaging through Pierre's refrigerator.

"Honestly," Pierre said, running his hand over his fade. "Me neither."

They both laughed.

"So what's up? What's the game?"

Pierre tapped his hands against his kitchen island and sighed. "She got under my skin."

"Sage seems like she gets under everyone's skin."

He laughed. "True...but something about it...her...I want her."

"Get that twinkle out your eye," Julian said. "Chicks can smell fear a mile away."

"Fear? What? Julian, shut up. I ain't scared of that girl."

"Yeah, okay."

Pierre sighed, deciding not to confess too much to his cousin. He didn't want to admit that he was feeling Sage as much as he was. He hadn't even known it. When they met he was annoyed by the situation and had taken his frustrations out on her. Sage stood up to him, she was professional, and she was passionate about her business.

She was still annoying. Pierre made the mistake of following her on social media and then she became...less annoying. Their obvious connection through music had sparked his interest in a more positive way. He was always taught to follow his instincts.

"So where are you taking her?" Julian asked.

"Who told you that you could eat my leftovers?" Pierre asked, frowning. Julian waved him off.

"You don't even eat them," he said. "Answer the question."

"I got a few ideas."

"A few ideas? Didn't you say the date tomorrow? You should have this planned out by now."

"It ain't that serious," Pierre said, not wanting to get too excited just in case things didn't go well.

"Fool, you ain't that serious. Just call it off. Save yourself the embarrassment."

Pierre looked at him. "Get out."

Julian laughed. "I can't wait to hear about this date," Julian said, picking up his to-go plate as he walked out of the kitchen. Pierre shook his head as he heard his front door close.

"Maybe he's right," he thought.

Pierre went over all his interactions with Sage thus far. From their rocky introduction and her pushy business practices to her assumptions about him as a man. He thought about their bond over music and how their conversations the last few days had been the highlight of his days. He was in no way ready to tell her that, but he did want to make a good impression on their first date.

Pierre silently cursed. He hadn't even thought much about it other than wanting to spend time with her. He was usually on top of things, but ever since their direct message conversation, Pierre just felt drawn to her. Now just the idea of a basic dinner date didn't seem like enough. He had to think and think fast.

"This playlist is perfect," Sage sighed, somewhat disappointed that Pierre had pegged her so well yet again. She hated to admit that there were only three songs on it that she didn't already have in her playlist. After listening to them, she added them immediately.

"What are you talking about?" Carmen asked, pushing Sage's arm to knock her from her thoughts. Sage looked over at her best friend and sighed.

"Sorry love, you pick a movie?"

"I asked you what you frowned up about?"

"Do you think agreeing to that date with Pierre was a mistake?" Sage blurted out. Carmen frowned.

"No," she said, immediately. "You clearly think he's attractive."

"Yeah, but I feel like we'd argue a lot. Plus isn't it wrong to mix business with pleasure?"

"You're contracted for a short period of time, you're not one of his employees," Carmen pointed out. "And you clearly love to argue."

Sage gasped. "Why would you say such a thing?"

Carmen chuckled. "Because you do, boo. It's your foreplay. You get off on it." Sage didn't respond. "When is the date anyway?"

"Tomorrow."

"Girl! Why are we talking about this? We need to figure out what you're going to wear."

"I don't even know where he's taking me."

"You don't need to know. You know how to step out on the first date," Carmen said. "Don't act brand new. Let's go."

"Where?"

"The closet!" Carmen said, getting up. "Now!"

Sage huffed but followed Carmen to her closet. She'd never prepared for a date this early in advance, but she had to admit that she was nervous.

The next evening, Sage was surprised when Pierre rang her doorbell on time. She decided against mentioning it just as she opened the door for him.

"You're ready?" Pierre asked with a confused look on his face.

Sage smirked, but nodded. "You said 7, right?"

Pierre returned her gesture. "Yeah, I did...You look beautiful."

Sage smiled. She tried hard not to dress too professionally, but she wanted him to know she knew this was a date and not a business meeting. Her red blouse had a blue, white and pastel yellow floral print on it and the v cut in the front showed just enough. Her red trousers had an attached scarf belt that she knotted but let the ends fall and fit her hips perfectly, but flared out to lay over her heels. She tried something different with her hair, letting Carmen put finger waves in it. Her makeup was light but she did get a fill on her lash extensions that morning. "Thank you."

He stepped aside to let Sage walk ahead of him. She closed and locked her door before making her way down the sidewalk path. He was parked a few spaces down from her, but before Sage could get to the door, he came from around her to open it.

"Thank you," she said, softly. After making sure she was in and the door was closed, Pierre slowed his strides to get around to his side. He had to admit that her being on time and looking as good as she did had won major points with him.

"Pace yourself," he thought before opening his door. Sage looked at him and smiled. Once he started the car, she smiled harder to hear a familiar Sir song.

"Are you trying to butter me up?" Sage asked, buckling her seatbelt.

"I might be," he replied, backing out of her parking lot. She only nodded and swayed in her seat to the song. "You're not going to ask where we're going?"

"...Where are we going?"

"I'm not telling you."

Sage frowned. "So why tell me to ask?"

"Just figured you would," he said. Sage snickered.

"You're so sure you know me, Pierre. I'm full of surprises."

He eyed her suspiciously, but Sage saw the hint of a smile. "Looking forward to being surprised."

Sage shut up at his flirtatious tone and just enjoyed not driving for once.

It was March now, but the air only had a slight chill to it that evening. Pierre had his sunroof halfway back, but his heat was on. Sage sighed as the air hit her body. She relaxed into the leather seat before turning to look at her date for the evening.

"So what made you ask me out?" Sage asked. Pierre glanced at her before looking back at the road.

"If I would have known you'd get this pretty for me, I would have asked weeks ago."

She smirked. "You saying I haven't been pretty any other time you've seen me?"

"You know that's not what I'm saying."

Sage nodded. "I do, but that didn't answer my question."

"I have my reasons." Pierre reached over with his right hand and interlaced his fingers with her left. Sage gasped at the contact, but decided that she liked it. "What matters is what I do with them right?"

"Right," she whispered, exhaling to calm herself.

"Now can you just sit pretty for me for a minute and enjoy the evening?" Sage playfully rolled her eyes, but nodded and smiled.

"I guess I can manage that."

"You guess huh?" Pierre said, laughing. "You really something else."

Sage smirked as she hummed along to the song playing. "I really do love this album."

"So I've been told."

Sage noticed their drive was a little long, but decided she didn't totally hate it. She usually fell asleep when anyone else was driving, but she wanted to stay alert so she could pay attention and stay engaged in their conversation. They talked about everything but work until Pierre pulled up at their destination.

Cooper Hawk Winery.

"Oh, I haven't been here in a while," Sage smiled.

Pierre licked his bottom lip. "Come on. We have a wine tasting before dinner."

Sage's eyes widened in surprise. "Really?"

"I don't just drink Hennessy, Sage," Pierre teased. "I'm a classic man."

Sage laughed before gathering her clutch and following Pierre out of the car. He reached for her hand when they got around the car and ushered her to the inside of the sidewalk. Sage took a deep breath, trying not to get excited with all the little points Pierre was scoring. He wasn't supposed to make her feel any type of way, especially not before her first glass of wine for the evening.

"I hope they still have their shrimp and polenta dish."

Pierre held the door to the restaurant open for Sage to walk in first. A short woman just inside of the second set of doors had a round serving tray with a few glasses of a white wine.

"Welcome to Cooper Hawk Winery."

"Thank you," Sage said, as she tucked her clutch under her arm and took two of the glasses, handing one to Pierre.

"Where do we check in for private wine tastings?" Pierre asked and the short woman smiled.

"Right over there with the cashier near the dessert display."

"Thank you," Pierre said. He sipped his wine before placing his free hand on the small of Sage's back. She took that as her que to walk as they made their way over to the cashier. Pierre checked them in for their reservation as Sage looked around. The dimly lit restaurant definitely gave a nice first date vibe.

"It smells good in here," she said as Pierre walked around and stood close in front of her. She gasped and held on to her wine glass as he leaned in closer to her neck.

"You smell better."

"...Thank you," she whispered, moving back to take a sip of her wine. She looked at him through the glass. Pierre was an attractive man. He towered over Sage's short frame. His brown skin was just about flawless and Sage could tell he was letting his beard grow. His slanted eyes were a lighter brown than his skin. His teeth are what did it though. Pierre had a very handsome smile. He was slim, yet muscular and Sage loved how he wore his suits. He hadn't been in one that particular night, but his outfit was nice. He had on jeans and a beige sweater with a white button down under it, only visible around his collar and at the bottom of the shirt. His boots were the same color as his sweater with patches of darker brown on them. Sage could tell he had gotten a haircut. His waves were clean. "I feel like this date is calculated."

"It is," he said, chuckling as he licked his lips. "But not how you're thinking."

"Um hum."

Pierre chuckled. "I just want to have a good time with you, all work aside, and get to know the real Sage better."

"The real Sage is who you see when I'm at work," she said. "I don't code switch." She shifted her weight from one heel to the other.

"I've seen professional Sage," he countered with a raised eyebrow and a playful smile. "There has to be more there."

"There is."

"I'd like the privilege of seeing that side."

Sage swallowed her wine slowly, their banter had stirred something inside of her. She wanted to keep it up, but found Pierre played the game too well. "Privileges have to be earned," she whispered, trying her hand at getting the last word.

Pierre stepped just an inch closer to her, causing Sage to inhale. "I'm sure you know by now that I'm not a man who is afraid of a little hard work."

Sage closed her mouth as quickly as she had opened it. Her skin felt hot as she looked up into Pierre's eyes, challenging him in that moment. When he smirked, Sage knew that he silently accepted the challenge and planned on winning.

"Harris!" The hostess called. They both turned and walked back to the desk and followed the hostess to the back room where the private wine tasting was held. Sage made a mental note to pace herself with the wine. There was no way Pierre would be getting into her bed tonight. That was for sure.

After their wine tasting, the two were escorted to their booth in the restaurant part of the winery. Pierre had purchased a bottle of some sweet wine he liked during the tasting and the waitress brought it out with a fancy decanter and two wine glasses.

"You come here often?" Sage asked.

"I've been once or twice," he said. "It's been a while though."

"You bring all your first dates here?"

"Usually only third dates if they're lucky." Sage frowned and he laughed. "I'm kidding, Sage."

"Right," she said, sitting back to look at the menu.

"Do you two need a moment to look at the menu or are you ready to order? Maybe an appetizer?

"Do you see what you want?" Pierre asked Sage.

She smiled and did a little dance in her seat. "They have the shrimp and polenta!"

"I'm assuming that's what you want?" the waitress asked. "It's so good."

"Yes, I'll have that."

"I want the ginger soy glazed New York strip, medium well."

"The potatoes and grilled vegetables, okay?"

"Yes."

"Great!" The waitress said. "I'll put your orders in right away."

"So, Mr. Harris," Sage said once the waitress walked away. "What are your intentions?"

Pierre raised an eyebrow. "With you?"

"And in general, with dating."

"It's been sporadic the last few months due to work and just not feeling the scene, but I would like to settle down soon. What about you?"

"I have chosen to date with intention," she said. "I don't need any more mindless situationships."

"You don't even strike me as the kind to play like that."

"I'm not," Sage said. "I'm focused on building my legacy. I'd love to find a man who is doing the same."

"You want to build a legacy?"

Sage nodded. "That's the plan. I plan to train other consultants soon and start an agency."

"That's dope," Pierre said. "Replicate and expand."

Sage smiled. She loved that she didn't have to explain being an entrepreneur to him. "Exactly."

"Makes sense. Have to work smarter and not harder," he said. "That's how I felt when I bought my second truck and put someone else in the first one. I was tired of running up and down the highway and not being able to do other things."

"Was trucking always something you wanted to do?"

Pierre shook his head. "Nah. I had no idea what I wanted to do until after high school. One of my boys got locked up and I realized hanging out with them and doing what we did wasn't working out. I looked into freight and found out how much I could make and it just took off from there."

"I'll admit that I love how ambitious you are," Sage said. Pierre's eyebrows raised at the confession. "Even with just looking at your reports and your brand I can tell you really love what you do."

"Thanks," he said. "But I don't want to talk about work anymore."

The waitress came back out with their food, each of them taking a moment to prepare it before Pierre blessed the table. Sage groaned inwardly. Pierre was winning this date and the vulnerability she felt almost made her sick.

"So what do you want to talk about?" Sage asked.

"Do you cook?" he asked. She laughed at the random question.

"I've recently gotten more into it," she answered. "Especially since my mom moved back home."

"Y'all not from here?" he asked.

Sage shook her head. "I am, but my grandmother is from Charlotte."

Pierre nodded. "I've been there a few times."

"I don't go as often as they would like," she admitted.

"Why not?"

Sage sighed, thinking of her brother. "Just busy, I guess."

"I feel it," Pierre said. Sage smiled.

The two enjoyed the rest of their date getting to know each other outside of work. Sage's apprehension about dating Pierre slipped as the night progressed. Just like their DM conversation, it was easy and fluid. It made Sage wonder if they really could be something outside of associates.

It was a little after 11p when Pierre pulled back into Sage's apartment complex. She was tired, but found she didn't want to leave him so soon. She sighed, chastising herself for even having thoughts of inviting him in.

Sage waited until she had unlocked her door, pushing it ajar just enough to see inside, before turning to Pierre.

"Did you enjoy our first date?" he asked with a smile that made Sage sway just a little.

"I did," she said. "Thank you."

He grabbed her hand and ran his thumb over her knuckles. "When can I see you again?"

"We have an appointment on Wednesday, correct?" she asked.

Pierre chuckled and shook his head. "Not professionally, Sage."

"Oh," she said. "Second date vibes already?" She teased him, wearing a smirk.

"Cut it out," he said. "Answer the question."

Sage smiled. "That's your call."

"My call?" Pierre asked, leaning over to push Sage's door open. He helped her up into her door and stepped back into his position. "I like the sound of that."

Sage smirked. "Yeah?" he nodded. "Well use the upper hand wisely. I don't give it away too often."

Eight

Pierre didn't waste time with his advantage. A few days later, he was ringing Sage's doorbell for their official second date. Sage smiled, feeling giddy as she opened her front door to see a bouquet of flowers.

"Oh, I like this second date already," she said, grabbing at the roses before stepping aside.

"I love that you're always ready when you say you'll be," Pierre said, leaning in to kiss her cheek. Sage blushed.

"Come in, let me put these in water before we leave."

Pierre nodded before following Sage into her apartment. He didn't want to mention that this was his first time inside. He noticed how comfortable she was with him in that moment and he didn't want to disrupt it. So, he followed her closely through the foyer and into the kitchen. Looking around, he found her place decorated as expected. It fit her. She used a lot of earth tones with bursts of orange and green to accent everything. He knew she'd have a lot of plants which is why he brought flowers in the first place. Her place had a comforting appeal to it. It was cool and held a lot of natural light.

"Hmm," she said, smelling the flowers. "These smell so good. I usually get fresh flowers for my table. Thank you for saving me a trip."

"My pleasure."

"Are you going to tell me why I'm wearing sneakers on a date?"

"You said you wanted to do something fun," he said. "We're going to Dave and Buster's."

"Yes! I knew it!" she said, shuffling back and forth on her feet. Pierre laughed as she threw her arms halfway up and did a little wiggle. "I'm excited. Let's go."

"That wasn't the response I was expecting," he said, following her back to the door. Sage turned to him and smirked. Pierre restrained himself from pulling her into a kiss.

"You're so sure you know me, P."

"I'm getting there."

The two made small talk until Pierre pulled up into the parking lot of Dave and Buster's.

"Are we eating here?"

"I have something else planned for dinner, if you don't mind."

"I'm good with whatever you have planned." Pierre looked at her. "What?"

"You feeling me, huh?" he asked. Sage's eyes grew wide.

"I mean we are on a date, Pierre."

"I'm just saying," he chuckled. "You going along for my plans is proof. I know you love to be in control."

Sage rolled her eyes. "Professionally, yes I do like to be in control. It's why I own my own business. In relationships, I have no problem letting a man be a man."

Pierre smiled, turning off the car. "Good to know."

He got out first, walking around to open Sage's door. She smiled as he grabbed her hand and they made their way into the building. There was a line at the counter, but Pierre led them straight past the dining area and into the game room.

Sage looked around while he purchased a power card. It was early afternoon and although there were a lot of kids around, it wasn't too crowded at the time.

"Every time I come they rearrange these games," Sage said. Pierre nodded, handing her a card. She eyed him while he put both hands behind his back, leaning forward and smiling. "What are you up to?"

"Care to bet?" he asked, licking his lips.

Sage smirked, crossing her hands under her chest. "On?"

"Who gets the most tickets."

"What's the wager?"

"Lady's choice."

"Um," Sage said, biting her lip while looking around at the games. "How about a blind bet?"

Pierre stuck his right hand out. "Challenge accepted."

While Pierre stopped at each game that looked interesting to try his hand, Sage made a plan on which machines would get her the most tickets. She remembered one game in particular, a fish game similar to the wheel of fortune wheel, that she would play with her brother. She found it next to the basketball game that Pierre was currently at.

"I'm definitely going to win," she thought, sliding the card and waiting for the light to turn green.

About an hour later, Sage wanted to call it quits because she was hungry. Pierre agreed but wanted to play one more game on the way to the winner's circle.

"I think I know what I'm going to make you do," she said, smiling. He stopped at a small, round game with laser lights spinning in a circle.

"You won't have the chance," he teased, watching the light go around a few times. Sage rolled her eyes but her mouth dropped when he landed on the jackpot. "Check me out!"

Sage stomped her foot, watching as he collected his tickets. "How did you do that?"

Pierre smirked, grabbing her hand to walk to the winner's circle. "Just be ready to do what I say."

"Umm, that still doesn't mean you beat me," she said, handing the cashier her card. They both watched the screen in anticipation.

"You have 1,321 tickets," she said, handing Sage the card. She smiled.

"Thank you." Sage turned to watch Pierre as he handed the cashier his card.

"You have 1,823 tickets."

"I need a recount," Sage said. The cashier laughed as she handed Pierre his card back.

"Come on, loser," he said, pulling her through the metal detector. "I'll spend my tickets on you."

Sage pouted. "I can't believe I lost."

Pierre laughed before he began looking around. He helped Sage pick out all the things she wanted. They grabbed a neon orange water bottle with the Dave and Buster's logo, a plush rolling eyes emoji pillow, a jumbo pen, and a bunch of candy before they went to the register and checked out. Sage had to admit that even though she lost, she was having a great time with Pierre.

They had a few coins left, so they stopped at a shooting game and a racing game on the way out.

"I'm hungry now."

"I'm going to feed you," he said as they left the building. "Since this is our official second date, it's two parts to it," Pierre said.

"You didn't get enough of me beating you in those last few games?" Sage asked.

"I enjoyed watching you have fun," Pierre said. Sage stopped laughing and blushed.

"That was smooth," she said, stepping aside to let him open the car door.

"And it got you to be quiet," he said. "Two points for me."

Sage laughed as she secured her seatbelt in Pierre's passenger seat. She waited for him to get around to his side. "So what's the second part of our date?"

"It's at my place," he replied. "I want to show you something."

Sage frowned, raising her eyebrow. "What do you need to show me at your place?"

Pierre looked at her for a moment, realizing what she was insinuating and laughed. "Not like that. Get your mind out of the gutter."

Sage sighed in relief. "I just wanted to make sure. Our day was going so well."

"It still is," he said, licking his lips while running his thumb over her hand. Sage tried not to blush. "Plus, you lost the bet."

Sage rolled her eyes. "So where do you stay?"

"You heard of Mansions on the Plaza? It's off..."

"I know where it is," Sage said. "Impressive."

"I do okay," Pierre said with a smirk.

"I've seen your books."

He laughed before telling her he'd let her pick the music while he drove. Sage smiled before taking his phone and scrolling through his music.

"You named a playlist after me?" Sage asked.

"It's the songs I sent you."

"I see, but...you named it after me."

"Girl chill...it's a public Apple Music playlist...not a prenup," he said, smirking.

Sage laughed before hitting him in his arm. "Always talking mess."

"I always wondered what the inside of these looked like," Sage said, running her finger over the marble of his kitchen island."

"You can admire it later," he said. "I need your help."

"When you said the second part of our date was here, I figured you were cooking for me."

"We can order in," he said, grabbing her hand and leading her down the hallway. He opened up a door to what seemed to be his home office. Sage frowned to see boxes of school supplies, toiletries, and bags everywhere.

"Who did you rob?" Sage asked, crossing her arms over her chest. Pierre laughed.

"Sage, be for real. You said it yourself...you've seen my books."

"Touche," Sage said, throwing her hands up. "But what's up?"

"I usually have these bags put together by now but I've been putting it off. The company donates school supply bags and care packages every year."

"Oh cool," Sage said, smiling. "Who are they for?"

"We spread them out over a few organizations, depending on how much we have. So you're helping me package them."

"This is your wager?" Sage asked. Pierre nodded. "Well, I definitely always pay my debts."

Pierre smiled. "Good. What would you like for dinner?

"Italian please. No tomato sauce."

He nodded. "I'll be right back."

Sage looked around while kicking her shoes off. She pushed them into a corner and sat her purse on top of them before deciding to tackle the toiletries first. It looked a bit more organized than the school supplies and the bags weren't so big.

Pierre came back in with a bottle of wine and two glasses. "Food should be here within the hour."

"Sounds good." she smiled down at the pile of hand sanitizers when she heard music come through a speaker from his desktop computer. "So you said you do this every year?"

"Yeah, something my mom suggested and we just kind of ran with it. It's not much, but it helps."

66

"It does," Sage said, nodding. "You have me thinking about the last time I've donated or volunteered."

"See, you thought I was just some conceited dude who was only in it for the money," Pierre said, smiling at his victory of surprising Sage with a different side of him. She tossed up both her hands.

"You're right. I'll admit I thought you were a bit of a narcissist."

"...I wasn't going to go that far," he said. Sage giggled.

"I apologize. This is really nice what you're doing."

"Thanks. I've done it every year since I've made a profit. Don't like to broadcast it but I appreciate the help. Usually my cousin and a few interns do this. Thanks for the free labor."

"You'll pay one way or the other," Sage teased. Pierre laughed before continuing to stuff a bag.

"That sounds like something my dad would say. 'Everything has a price and it ain't always money.'"

"That is a fact," Sage said, giggling.

"I hated it growing up, but I learned to appreciate all the little nuggets he drops on a daily basis."

"You and your dad are close like that?" Sage asked. Pierre nodded and smiled.

"He's my best friend," he said. Sage smiled. "Why you look like that?"

"No reason...just nice to see."

"You and your dad close?"

"....We used to be."

"What happened?" Pierre asked. Sage stopped packing the bag she was on, but continued to look down. She wasn't sure why, but she felt comfortable enough to give Pierre the short version of her family dysfunction. "You don't have to tell me if..."

"No, it's okay," Sage said, giving him a smile as reassurance to her words. "Um...a few years ago, my brother was killed.

Random shooting at some club downtown. He wasn't the intended target but...you know how that goes."

"I do," Pierre said, stopping his movements as well, giving Sage his attention. "I'm sorry to hear that."

Sage sighed. "His death really took a toll on all of us. My parents couldn't stand each other. Daddy kind of checked out when it happened. He was there physically, but mentally...he left us all. Their marriage didn't make it a year after my brother was buried. My sister defends him saying we all have to grieve in our own ways. I get it but I just don't think his way is very productive."

"Not everything is goal-driven, Sage. Some things just happen."

"It should be," she spoke quickly. "If not, then what's the point?"

"So what would you say the point of this is?" he asked.

"Of what?"

"Us...dating?"

"We're dating?"

"This a date ain't it?"

Sage fought not to roll her eyes. "Dating has a point."

"I didn't ask you what dating's point is," he said. "I said, what's the point of us dating?"

"What's the difference?"

"You know the difference," he said, leaning closer to her.

"I'm not sure yet," she whispered. "And that bothers me."

Pierre rubbed his nose against hers. Sage closed her eyes. "If it makes you feel any better I don't either," they both laughed. "It's a feeling though right? A vibe?"

"That could mean a lot of different things."

"Sometimes you should just be quiet and feel it," Pierre said. Sage nodded right before he kissed her softly. "There's always a point to your feelings," he said against her lips before kissing her again. She placed her hand on his cheek and kissed him back.

"Feelings get you in trouble," she still tried to protest. Pierre pushed on the small of her back, moving her closer so he could kiss her deeper. Sage sank into the embrace.

"Shut up sometimes," he said. Sage laughed before Pierre kissed her again.

Nine

Realizing there was only a week left in her company's guarantee, Sage had to pump the breaks on her budding romance with Pierre. It was the last thing she wanted to do, but now more than ever, she was invested in finding the issues that were stopping his company from growing and moving forward.

Carmen was over cooking dinner for her, while Sage had all of her work spread across the dining room table.

"I made you some tea," Carmen said.

"Thank you," Sage said. "I think I have it narrowed down to the issue, but trying to figure out how they're losing money on basic stuff is weird."

"You think someone's stealing from him?" Carmen asked.

"Hopefully it's just clerical errors," Sage said, rubbing her forehead. "I'd hate someone to get fired."

"Well, if that's what happens, that's what happens. You just have to do your job, love."

Sage nodded. "You're right. Food smells good though."

Carmen smiled. "Baked chicken alfredo and garlic bread."

"Let me get this work done before you put me into a food coma."

Carmen laughed as she got up to check the food. Sage's phone buzzed and she sighed to see Pierre calling her after she'd ignored his text message.

"You're tired of me already?"

Sage giggled. "Oh, just the opposite. Trying to get my work done so I'll have more time for you."

"I like the way that sounds," he said. "But how long do I have to wait?"

"You do remember the contract we signed right?"

"That was before…" Sage smiled. He didn't have to finish his sentence because she knew exactly what he meant. "Well, since I can't see you, can you at least give me an update?"

"Everything will be in my report, love."

"Fine," he huffed. Sage tried to hold her laugh in. "I see you aren't willing to compromise here."

Sage bit her lip. "How about I FaceTime you after my bath?"

"During sounds better."

"Pierre!"

He chuckled. "Fine. See you later."

Sage sighed, hating to even hang up on him. "See you later."

Sage hung up her phone and laughed to see Carmen fake gagging.

"I'm going to be sick," she teased. "You make me sick!"

"I feel a little sick myself," Sage said. "This feeling scares me, Car."

Carmen sighed, sitting next to her best friend and patting her knee. "It's okay to be a little hesitant, it makes you aware and alert."

Sage waited for her to continue. "But?"

"Don't block your blessings."

Sage laughed. "Okay, pastor."

"The Lord said there is a ram in the bush!" Carmen said, standing up and throwing her right hand up, spreading her fingers and waving her hand. "Hallelujah!"

Sage giggled at her friend, but kept what she said in mind.

This was dangerous territory she was in with Pierre Harris. The fact that it had only been a couple of weeks since they'd met was not lost on Sage in the slightest. Her mind screamed it to her heart every time it began to beat a little faster in his presence. It wasn't sensible; to like someone this much so quickly. Sage felt fear at the fact that she knew this and still hadn't fought against the feeling. She welcomed it. How foolish did that make her?

Sage thought about Pierre all while finishing her work for the day and through dinner. Their text conversations, phone calls, dates, everything flooded her memory while her heart and mind battled each other. Sage was a logical person. She was keen on doing her research, laying out all variables and finding the best solution for everything. Her feelings for Pierre in such a short time were a problem for her. She didn't trust them, yet she couldn't shake them and that was insane to her.

Once Carmen left, Sage had reached a breaking point in her mental war. Instead of calling Pierre, she sent him a message and asked him if he would come over. It was almost 11pm, but Sage had to see him. He responded back that he would be there as soon as he could. She jumped up, looking around to make sure her apartment was presentable before going to freshen up.

Sage changed into a satin lounge set that wasn't too revealing, but cute nonetheless. It was emerald color and the pants had a black lace pattern up the sides of the leg that also went around the edges of the camisole. She removed her scarf from her head, brushing her hair down to lay flat against her scalp. After washing her face, she went to find a nice bottle of wine to open.

Pierre knocked on her door before she finished her first glass.

"Coming!" Sage called out, taking a moment to finish her glass before going to the door. Pierre smiled when she did. "Hey."

"What's up?" he asked, not hiding the fact that he eyed her from head to toe. Sage blushed a little before moving to let him in.

"Thanks for coming."

"Thank you for inviting me," he said, turning to hug her. Sage melted into his embrace before stepping back to shut and lock her door.

"Would you like some wine?"

"Got anything stronger?" he asked. Sage giggled and replied in the negative. "Then wine is fine."

"Good," she said, walking into her kitchen to grab another glass. Pierre followed, sitting down at her island.

"You started without me?" he teased, pointing at her glass. "Possibly."

He watched her bring the glass over to him and pour wine into it. "So what do I owe the pleasure of this night cap?"

"Honestly?" Sage said, reaching over to pour another glass for herself. She was standing in front of him, but Pierre placed his hand on her hip and moved her just a little closer. "I couldn't stop thinking about you since our call earlier and I decided FaceTime wasn't going to work for me."

Pierre smiled, satisfied with her answer. "So you needed some real face time?"

"I did."

Pierre kept her in place with one hand while leaning back against the back of the stool to sip his wine. Sage allowed him a moment to get his thoughts together. Even with all of the time they had been spending together, she had never been this forward.

She had never seen him this casual either. He had on a pair of red sweatpants and a black long sleeve tee. The Nikes he had on reminded Sage of a pair that her brother used to wear a lot. That made her smile a little.

"Are you finally ready to admit that you're feeling me as much as I'm feeling you?" he asked. Sage frowned.

"You haven't admitted such a thing so what does that mean?"

"I've shown you."

"And I believe I've shown you," she retorted. Pierre sighed, noticing her agitation.

"Not really...but chill," he said, putting his glass down on the counter and sliding his free hand on her other hip. He sat up again and hugged her, rubbing his hands up and down her back. Sage almost hated that it calmed her down. "We're just talking. No need to get ready for war."

Sage sighed. "Let's go to the living room."

Pierre nodded, grabbing his glass and the bottle of wine before following Sage into the living room. Letting him sit down first, Sage tried to put a little distance between them. Pierre chuckled before putting his wine glass down on the coffee table, wrapping his arm around her waist and pulling her closer.

"How was your day?" he asked. Sage sighed at his comforting tone.

"It was productive, but long. Yours?"

"About the same." Pierre framed her face with his hand. "You are beautiful."

"Thank you," she whispered.

"Especially when you aren't trying to argue with me."

Sage rolled her eyes. "Don't ruin the moment."

He laughed. "I'm just saying, you do it a lot."

"I just want to make sure my point is conveyed and understood." She took his hand from her face, interlacing her fingers with his as it fell to her knee. She looked down at their hands together and bit her lip.

"I hear you," he said. Sage looked up just as Pierre leaned in to kiss her. Pierre gripped the side of her neck as their kiss deepened. Sage held on to his wrist, running her thumb over it as she encouraged his movements.

"Can you tell me why I like you so much after only two weeks?" he asked against her lips. Sage smiled.

"Because I'm pretty awesome."

"I agree with that."

"Finally! We agree on something." Laughter interrupted their kiss as Sage pushed her shoulder into her couch. She smiled at Pierre as his eyes roamed over her face. "I am feeling you as much as you're feeling me."

Pierre smiled, satisfied with her confession. "Now that we got that out of the way…"

He leaned back in, pushing his lips into hers. Sage giggled before reciprocating the kiss.

"I didn't call you over here just to make out, I promise."

"I don't mind."

She laughed. "I just wanted to chill and get to know you more."

Pierre sighed, taking the hint and sitting back against the arm of the couch. He grabbed his glass of wine. "What do you want to know?"

"Thank you for being a gentleman," she said.

"You don't have to thank me for that. My old lady raised me right."

"Well then, I can't wait to thank her for that."

Pierre smirked. "Keep looking at me like that and you won't have anything to thank her for."

Sage felt her neck to see if it was hot before putting her glass of wine down. "I changed my mind. Let's watch a movie."

He chuckled. "Lady's choice."

Sage smiled, grabbing the remote before folding her legs under her body and leaning into his side. Pierre relaxed, wrapping one arm around her shoulders, and finished his glass while Sage picked a movie.

Ten

Working from a home office had its benefits. Sage didn't have to get dressed if she didn't want to and she set her own hours. She could listen to music or podcasts as loud as she wanted. She didn't have to worry about nosy co-workers or annoying bosses. Overall, she loved working for herself. One thing she hated though was when house issues became work issues.

Last night after a storm knocked her power out, she hadn't been able to get any work done that morning. She was only grateful that she didn't have much food in her refrigerator to worry about it spoiling.

Sage wondered whose house she would crash for the day just as her phone rang. She smiled to see Pierre calling.

"Good morning," she sang sweetly, rolling her eyes at her own tone. She was too giddy about Pierre's phone call, but decided she didn't mind the feeling.

"Good morning," he said. "I miss my wake up call this morning?"

Sage blushed. She had been calling him the last few mornings since their second date. She didn't think it meant that much to him.

"I'm sorry. My power went out last night so I'm trying to figure out what to do."

"It isn't back on? They're sending someone out to work on it?" he asked. Sage closed her eyes at his concern.

"Not until later," Sage answered. "I'll proba…"

"Come to my place," he said. Sage blinked as she looked up at her ceiling.

"Aren't you working today?"

"I was headed in later, but I don't have to."

"I don't want to impose."

Pierre sighed. "I offered, didn't I?" Sage didn't respond. "I want you to come over here."

Sage closed her eyes, finally welcoming the warmth in her heart. "Okay."

"Would it make you feel better if I let you cook for me?"

Sage rolled her eyes, but laughed. "What do you want to eat?"

"Oh, I was joking but I'll take whatever your best dish is."

"You aren't ready for my best dish," Sage teased. "But I'll think of something."

"What time are you coming?"

"I'm getting dressed now."

About an hour later, Sage pulled up to Pierre's apartment, eager to spend the day with him. She couldn't even remember the last time she spent the day with a man. It had to be after her ex, but she wasn't sure if it was within the last year. Pushing aside how uneventful her love life was, Sage sent Carmen a text to let her know she made it. Sage called her after she agreed to Pierre's offer and Carmen was very excited about Sage spending the day with Pierre. She wanted to know all the details including when she got there.

Sage secured her car before going to knock. Pierre opened his front door before she could even knock.

"Good morning, again," he said, smiling as he took her bag from her.

Sage smiled. "Good morni…"

Before she could finish her greeting, Pierre had her wrapped in his arms. Sage's heart dropped a little as his hand pushed her lower back, bringing her chest to his. She looked up into his eyes just as he placed his lips on hers. Sage closed her eyes as he gave her a few more short, yet sweet kisses. "Good morning to you, too...again."

Pierre ran his nose over her neck and hugged her a little tighter. "You smell good."

Sage exhaled, hugging his shoulders and inhaling his scent as well. Any nervousness she felt coming over was completely gone. The comfort of his embrace was enough to ease her apprehensions.

Pierre pulled back and smiled before walking around Sage to close and lock his door.

She cleared her throat. "So...you want breakfast? Or...."

"We can wait until later," he said. "I know you have some work to get done and I'm almost done with this sermon I was listening to."

"Oh! Can I listen to the rest of it with you?" Sage asked. Pierre looked at her and nodded.

"Of course. My phone and some coffee are in the kitchen."

"Great."

After they listened to the sermon, both Pierre and Sage went into his home office to get some work done. He offered the desk to Sage, but she opted for the chair near the window, letting him keep his own work space. Pierre put on some jazz music and Sage fought against her smile. He had an old soul like her, but she hadn't expected him to play jazz while working. It wasn't something she did. She'd usually listen to jazz after getting all of her work done for the day, but Sage enjoyed this vibe and knew she'd have to incorporate jazz into her routine.

"I think I'm finally done for the day," she said, turning towards Pierre's desk. She frowned to see that he wasn't there. Sage's phone rang.

"You being decent over there?" Carmen asked. "Haven't heard from you since this morning."

Sage sucked her teeth. "Girl stop playing with me. We've just been working."

"Is that code for something?" Carmen teased. When Sage didn't respond, she laughed. "Okay let me stop. But for real. How's it going?"

"Surprisingly good. Now that I'm done working I'm looking forward to spending the day with him."

"What? You're admitting to that? I'm so proud of you, friend! Spend time with your man."

"...Why do you have to be so extra?"

"You wouldn't love me if I wasn't."

"Whatever," Sage said as she heard Pierre coming back down the hallway. "I'll call you later."

Sage hung up on Carmen just as Pierre came in. "You done working?"

She nodded. "I didn't even hear you leave."

"You were zoned out," he said. Sage laughed. "Is it my time now?"

He bit his lip when he said it. Sage knew it was intentional and the gesture did exactly what he wanted it to do. The urge to kiss him fell on her suddenly. Sage nodded while looking at Pierre's lips for a few more seconds.

"What do you plan on doing with your time?" she asked, smirking.

Pierre reached for her hand and pulled her out of the chair. She smiled up at him as he placed both of her hands around his neck and moved them around the chair.

"Are we dancing?" she asked. Pierre nodded.

"Yeah…going to dance you right to this kitchen," he said. Sage laughed but allowed him to move her out of the room. "I'm hungry."

"Are you going to help?"

Pierre frowned. "You said you were cooking for me!"

"At least stay in here and keep me company," she said, pouting. Pierre reached up and tapped her nose before kissing her.

"I can do that."

Sage let go of Pierre and turned towards the refrigerator, rubbing her hands together. "Okay, let's see what we got."

"The only thing unthawed is some fresh salmon," Pierre said, sitting at one of his island stools.

"How old is it?" Sage asked, frowning as she pulled it out. He laughed and told her it was only a few days old. "Okay cool. Protein picked." She looked through the drawers and saw a bag of brussel sprouts. "Got it. You have potatoes?"

"Instant?" he asked. Sage closed the refrigerator and frowned. "Then no."

"Okay, I need you to go to the store and get two potatoes, a small thing of heavy whipping cream, and some shredded parmesan cheese." Pierre took a note on his phone. "And a good bottle of wine."

He laughed. "Anything else?"

"No sir," she said, moving the brussel sprouts and salmon to the counter. "I'll find my way around."

Pierre smiled, deciding he liked the image of Sage finding her way around his kitchen. "I'll be right back."

By the time Pierre got back from the store, Sage had the brussel sprouts cut and cleaned and the salmon seasoned.

"Put me to work," Pierre said, handing her the bottle of wine to open.

"Rinse the potatoes off and poke some holes in them," she said, tasing the wine. "This is good!"

"I got skills, little momma," he said. Sage smiled while pouring him a glass. She had taken over his bluetooth speaker with her own music. Time by Sebastian Mikael came on and she couldn't help but sway to it. "Don't get tipsy over there now, you're still cooking."

Sage smiled. "Potatoes have to go in first. They'll take the longest."

They finished one bottle of wine while preparing their meal. Sage sautéed the sprouts on the stove before putting the whipping cream and cheese in the skillet and putting it in the oven on broil. She used Pierre's air fryer to grill the salmon. He opened the second bottle of wine as she plated their food.

"Never had Brussel sprouts like this," he said, sticking his fork in them. Sage smiled.

"Bless your table, sir," she said.

"You know I read a meme that said women only say sir when they like a man," he teased. "This is your second time saying it today." Sage blushed.

"Shut up and pray!" she said. They both laughed as Pierre held his hands out for her to grab.

"God, bless the hands that prepared this meal and the company you've blessed me with today. Amen."

Sage watched while Pierre took a bite of his food. She relaxed and smiled when he pushed his fork back into it and took another bite.

"I'll keep you around now," he said, nodding. "I approve."

Sage smirked. "I'm glad."

They talked about random things while eating their meal. Sage hadn't laughed that much about nothing in particular in a while. She couldn't believe she had been around him all day and still didn't want to leave. She said as much when Pierre asked her if she had anywhere she had to be. After they cleaned the kitchen together, Pierre grabbed their last bottle of wine and they headed into the living room to listen to some music and talk more.

"And as each morning brings a sunrise. And the flowers bloom in spring time. On my loving you can rely. I will stay with you."

Sage smiled as her shoulders dropped, pushing her body into the couch and closing her eyes to feel John Legend's voice. Pierre's thumb ran slowly over the knuckles on her left hand sending small shocks up her arm. It was a combination that forced her to relax.

"I loved this live version," she admitted. "Such a pretty song."

"Have you ever been in love like that?" Pierre asked, his voice almost as soft as the musician coming through his speaker. Sage shook her head.

"Not this deeply."

"Dance with me."

She opened her eyes to see if there was any hint of a joke on his face. Pierre hadn't even blinked. "What?"

"You heard me," he said. Sage giggled as he stood up from his couch. Swallowing her amusement, she looked up into his eyes and felt her heart open just a little. He leaned over, taking her hand yet waiting for her to grip his back before pulling her off the couch. Their eye contact did not falter as Pierre pulled her against his chest. She looked up at him and smiled as her chin rested against him. He chuckled.

"I really can't dance, so no clumsy jokes," she said. Pierre shook his head before framing her face with his hand. Sage sighed, wrapping both of her arms around him and pressing her hands flat against his back. They stayed silent for a verse, though Sage was sure he could hear her heart beating. Pierre kissed her every few seconds, lingering against her lips to prove his point. Sage was completely defeated and okay with it. Up until today, she had been throwing bricks at him in an attempt to guard her heart, but Pierre had dodged each one thus far. She relaxed more into his embrace and decided to accept it. "Thank you for today."

"You don't have to thank me," he said. Sage watched his Adam's apple move. "I enjoyed your company."

"And my food?" she smirked.

"That was a plus."

Sage laughed as Pierre moved them away from his coffee table so he could dance with her as he pleased. She ran her fingernails over his goatee and licked her lips.

"You're so handsome." Pierre's steps staggered and Sage laughed. "Really?"

"You ain't ever just came out and complimented me like that," he said. "You okay?" he teased, placing the back of his hand on her forehead. Sage laughed while swatting his hand away before going back to grip his goatee.

"Shut up," she said. "And kiss me."

Pierre obliged. "You aren't the boss of me."

Sage wrapped her arms around his neck as he bent down to kiss her again. "Yeah, okay."

Eleven

The weekend before Sage's final meeting with Pierre and his shareholders, he invited Sage to the company bbq. Sage didn't think much of it until he said his parents would be there as well. Not wanting to back out of accepting the invitation, Sage asked him if it would be okay for Carmen and Alondra to tag along. He said that was fine.

Pierre rented out a space in Tower Grove Park that had plenty of space, a gazebo, and a bbq grill. Sage didn't expect much for a BBQ, but it was set up really nice with a lot of company branding.

"This feels real official," Carmen said as the three of them walked up to the bbq. Alondra nodded.

"You two need to cut the extras and just enjoy the bbq," Sage said.

"You're about to meet his parents, sis," Alondra said. Sage rolled her eyes.

"This is literally a company thing. His company hired me. That's it, that's all." Sage hadn't told them about the last few times she spent with Pierre.

"Ugh, you are so annoying," Alondra said. "If you can't see how into you he is...you need help."

Sage sighed. "Listen, I'm just trying to focus on these last couple of days of my contract. Our meeting is this Tuesday. I feel like I'm missing something, but…"

"Nope!" Carmen said, popping the 'p' to cut her off. "Focus on that."

She pointed off to their left and all of them turned to look. Sage smiled as she saw Pierre smiling at her and waving her over. It was as casual as she had seen him dress, even more so than the night he came to her house. Pierre had on a fitted white tee that had the company's logo on it and a pair of black basketball shorts that reached his knees. Sage admired the way his muscles filled his tee and she had to admit that all thoughts of work ran out of her mind at record speed.

"I could use a break," she mumbled, biting her lip as she put a little speed in her walk. Alondra and Carmen hung back to tease her.

"She's open," Alondra said. "And I love it."

"Me too," Carmen said. They both laughed before catching up to her.

"What's up?" Pierre asked, hugging Sage. "You're always on time for everything."

She laughed. "Even bbqs…This is my sister, Alondra, and my best friend, Carmen."

Pierre nodded. "Nice to meet you ladies."

"Hi, Pierre," they said together. Sage frowned at them as Pierre just gave a confused smile.

"Um…okay," he said, laughing. "You ladies can have a seat anywhere you like. Once my dad gets here to pray over the food, we can eat."

The three began to walk off, but Pierre grabbed Sage's wrist. "What?"

"You can't go until you kiss me," he whispered. Sage blushed.

"In front of your employees?"

"Man, I'm the boss," he said. Sage laughed as he kissed her anyway. She ran her hand down his cheek.

"Do it again now because I'm not doing it in front of your parents."

Pierre kissed her again. "I'm not insane."

Sage laughed before he finally let her go.

As more people began to fall into the park, Sage enjoyed watching Pierre interact with them all. He was confident, yet comfortable with everyone. His employees and their families all had smiles on their faces and everyone seemed to be having a good time.

Sage, Alondra, and Carmen got up to fix their plates and when they came back to their table, Julian was sitting there with wine coolers.

"You ladies drinking?" he asked.

"I'll partake," Alondra said, picking one out first. "Thank you."

"This is Julian," Sage said. "This is my sister, Alondra, and best friend, Carmen."

Julian held his drink up to them. Three older people walked over and one of the men pushed Julian's shoulder.

"Get up and let these ladies sit down."

"Dang Uncle Jay," he said. "It's room."

Sage frowned. "Jay as in Jaren Harris?"

"The legend," he said. The woman with him rolled her eyes.

"Oh please," she said. "You must be Sage?"

"Yes, ma'am. Nice to meet you, Mrs. Harris."

"Call me Miss Janet."

"Jaren and Janet, that's so cute," Carmen said. Sage's eyes widened until Miss Janet smiled.

"I know, I picked good," she teased. They all laughed as everyone got comfortable at the table.

"This is Philip," Jaren said, pointing to the other man with them. "He's the company's operations manager."

"Oh!" Sage said. "I have a meeting with you on Monday."

"Let's get it over with," he said. Sage frowned, looking around.

"Excuse this grumpy old man," Miss Janet said. "No work today."

"It's always a good time to discuss work," Jaren said, chuckling. Miss Janet rolled her eyes and began to compliment Alondra on her curls. As they began their own conversation, Sage turned to Philip.

"I don't mind if you don't," she said. "I have my iPad in my car. It won't take long."

"Have at it," he said. Sage sighed before nodding and getting up, excusing herself from the table. While she was walking, Pierre came over to her and hugged her.

"You're leaving me already?" he asked. Sage blushed before putting her hand on his arm, yet stepping back a little.

"No, I just...Philip would rather do his interview now so I was going to get my…"

Pierre shook his head. "I didn't invite you here to work, Sage. I wanted to spend time with you."

Sage smiled up at him. She didn't like public displays of affection, especially when they weren't officially exclusive, but she placed her palm against his cheek.

"I know you didn't, but if he's comfortable with now so am I. Then you and I can have lunch together Monday instead. Just the two of us."

Pierre sighed, taking her hand and kissing the back of it. "Definitely could have been a lawyer."

Sage giggled before Pierre finally let her go. She jogged to her car, grabbed her iPad from the trunk, and headed back to the table. Sage spent the next 20 minutes talking to Philip before putting her work up and excusing herself again. She found Pierre playing a game with some of the employee's kids.

"It's my time now?" he teased. Sage laughed before she nodded.

"What are we playing?" she asked, sitting down on the blanket next to him.

"Some game Melissa made up and cheating in," Pierre said. The little girl with the bun on top of her head sitting across from him stuck her tongue out.

"No! You just don't know how to play."

"I told you to teach me," Pierre said. "I need help!"

"Teach me," Sage said. "I'll be on your team."

"He can't teach you," Melissa said, amusement playing on her innocent features. "He's losing."

Sage giggled until Pierre eyed her. She tossed her hands up and leaned back, laughing. "Sorry. Googly eyes? Never heard of it."

"You put the glasses on like this!" Melissa said, holding up a pair of round, purple glasses with yellow polka dots.

"You said you have to roll the dice first," Pierre said. Melissa rolled her eyes. "Duh, that's how you know what lens to use!"

Sage snickered. "So you roll the dice and where you land tells you which one of these to use to do what?"

"Draw a picture and your teammate has to guess what you are drawing," Melissa explained.

"Oh!" Sage said, waving her hand. "We got this!"

Pierre frowned. "We? I can't draw. Can you?"

Sage smiled at him. "We got this."

"Well you go first then since you're so confident," Melissa said. Sage eyed her and Pierre laughed, passing her the dice.

"Where's your partner?" Sage asked.

"I don't need one."

Sage looked at Pierre and he just laughed. Sage rolled and landed on the medium lens but she also had to draw with her right hand instead of her left.

Pierre noticed the anxiety on Sage's face and patted her knee. "You said we got this, remember?" he smiled. Sage playfully pushed his hand away before grabbing the paper. She put the glasses on and cursed under her breath. Pierre laughed before telling her to draw slow.

Thinking of the easiest way to draw her object, Sage started at the top with a triangle. She had no idea if it connected, but she drew a square under it.

"A house?" Pierre asked. Sage shook her head before closing her eyes and drawing an upside down L. Then moving back up to the top and drawing a cross.

"A church!" Pierre yelled. Sage dropped the pencil and tossed the glasses off.

"I told you! We got this!" she said. Melissa crossed her arms.

"That was too easy. That's only half a point."

"What!" Sage asked, looking at her in confusion. Pierre laughed, leaning over against the blanket and pushing the dice to Melissa.

"I told you she's cheating," he said. "It's cool though. I got a secret weapon now."

"Whatever," Melissa said. Sage laughed and moved a little closer to Pierre.

After the picnic, Sage got back into work mode. It was something that Philip said to her during the interview that made her revisit a few things in her research. Two days before their final meeting and she finally had a handle on where they were losing money. She spent those two days putting her presentation together and double checking her findings, so that she would be well prepared when meeting with Pierre and Julian.

Twelve

Day 21 of Sage's progressive guarantee came. She woke up that morning as she usually did, preparing for a presentation she'd given plenty of times. Sage couldn't deny the fact that this time was different. She'd fallen for Pierre in such a short amount of time and that it scared her. Wanting to not think about that today and focus on business was her top priority, but she was already failing.

"Get it together, Sage."

Following her normal routine, she grabbed her coffee and headed downtown. She was on autopilot until Nicole led her into the conference room she had become familiar with. She was almost done unpacking her things when Pierre looked inside the door.

"Good morning, beautiful," he said, coming to hug her.

"Good morning."

"We're actually going to be in my office,"

"Oh, okay…"

"Don't worry, the projector is up in there," he said. "I know you a little by now."

Sage playfully rolled her eyes. "Whatever."

Pierre helped her pack up her things before leading her to his office. He excused himself to get coffee while Sage went back to preparing for the meeting. Julian came in not too long after.

"Hey cousin," he joked.

"Don't start, Julian," Sage said. "Good morning."

"I hope you have good news for us," he said as Pierre walked back into the room.

Sage stood up straight and cleared her throat. "Well, it may not be good news, but it'll be informative and help Harris Trucking and Construction move forward."

"That's what we like to hear."

"During my evaluation period and even during the interview process with your management and supervisory team, it wasn't evident just where you guys were losing money. On paper, everything looks good. We did come up with a plan to target more luxury clientele with higher load rates for the trucking side. Also, developing more commercial and government relationships for the construction side to increase revenue. However, I wanted to be sure that all of your processes and procedures were cost effective as well to make sure that no unnecessary funds would be lost once your income increases. After much research and time analyzing the data, I found the problem."

"So there is a problem?" Julian asked. "Construction or trucking?"

"On the trucking side," Sage said, going to the next slide. "At the company picnic when I interviewed Philip, something he said didn't sit right with me."

"What did he say?" Julian asked. Sage idly wondered why Pierre hadn't said anything thus far, but she gave Julian her attention.

"He said that calculating fuel reimbursement was the easiest part of his job since all he had to do was use zip codes."

"That's how we track mileage," Pierre finally said. Sage nodded.

"Yes, it is in part, but looking over the rate confirmation sheets you gave me access to, I noticed that the shippers don't just use the zip codes. They use full addresses. They are paying based on exact miles. You are reimbursing your drivers using just the zip codes. It may take less time, but it's not accurate."

"Okay, that can't explain the total loss though," Pierre said. Sage sighed, trying not to notice his agitation. From spending so much time with him over the last few weeks, she was familiar with some of his mannerisms.

"It can," she said. "Using just the zip code just calculates it from the middle of that zip code. I went over just one month using the actual pick up and delivery addresses and look..." Sage pushed the button on her remote and moved to the next slide.

"Wow," Julian mumbled, sitting back in his chair. "That much in a month?"

"Just think of all he's missing out on just by taking the easy way to report."

"Sage," Pierre said. "Don't be disrespectful."

She frowned. "Disrespectful? I'm telling you that I've found the issue that will get your shareholders off your back and put money in your pocket and you're whining over my delivery? If I was a man this wouldn't even be a question."

"What?" Pierre looked at her confused. "What are you even talking about? I'm telling you that you're being disrespectful towards not only an employee but a family friend who I've known since I was younger."

"That doesn't excuse his mistakes," Sage said, cutting him off.

"And that doesn't excuse your attitude either," Pierre said. "If you can't be professional and cut all this extra stuff out, you can leave."

"Let's take a breather," Julian tried to interject.

"Are you seriously talking to me like that right now?" Sage asked.

"Is this all you found?" Pierre asked, not even looking at her anymore.

"Well, there are a few other things in my report…"

"We can read," Pierre said. "Julian will fulfill our end of the contract as agreed. You can leave."

Sage's skin felt red as she hurried to gather her things. She guessed she wasn't moving fast enough for him, because Pierre got up and left his office. Julian sighed.

"He'll calm down," he said. "I'll have him call you to apologize."

"You don't need to do that," Sage said. "We have nothing else to talk about. If you have any questions, you can email me. If we're good to go…"

"Of course," Julian said. "I just made the transfer to finish our payment to you. Thank you again. He might not like it, but it's the truth."

Sage nodded, somewhat justified but still heartbroken nonetheless.

Thirteen

The next day, Sage woke up with a headache akin to her hangover days. Her body felt as if she'd been in a fight so she cancelled her morning workout session and got back into bed. Grateful that she always took a few days off from work after a consultation ended, Sage wanted to lounge around all day and get over what happened and forget about Pierre.

Once she woke up again, she did her morning skin care routine slower than usual. She turned on her morning inspiration playlist, using her bluetooth speaker to put a little more bass into it. She was waiting for her mask to set when a song Pierre added to it began to play.

"Forget him," Sage said to herself. "If he can't see my value then that's his loss."

She quickly skipped the song and continued her routine.

Once she was done with that, Sage went into the kitchen to make a smoothie for breakfast. While gathering her fruits to rinse, she got a call from her father. She frowned, but answered quickly.

"Hey Dad. Is everything okay?"

"Everything's good baby girl, I was just calling to check on you."

"Oh...I'm...okay."

Donovan chuckled. "I just spoke with your sister so I figured I call and see if you would answer."

Sage sighed. "Daddy, I honestly don't know what to even say to you sometimes."

"I know, but this is a conversation we need to have in person. I'll be in town in a couple of weeks and would like to see you."

"In a couple of weeks? Why?"

"You know why."

Sage sighed before sitting down at her island. "You're coming to town for my birthday?"

"Yes. It's about time we fixed whatever is going on. I know it won't happen overnight, but we have to start."

"...Okay."

They talked for a little while longer before getting off the phone. Even though Sage had been upset about what happened yesterday with Pierre, talking to her dad felt like a huge weight lifted from her chest. She thought about what he said about nothing could be resolved over night and she wondered if she had been approaching business the wrong way. Although her 21-day guarantee looked good in promotions and marketing, was that realistic?

Maybe Pierre was right. Maybe the fuel loss wasn't that big of a deal. Maybe she had missed something. She hadn't been totally focused the last three weeks because of Pierre. However, that was no excuse. Sage decided she would never date a client again. It seemed like common sense now that she thought about it, but she had never been in that position before. She hadn't even liked Pierre as a person when they first met, how she ended up falling for him in such a short time was beyond her.

"That was just bad to begin with," Sage thought.

Deciding she needed to fall back into her normal routine as quickly as possible, Sage sent a text to Carmen to see if they wanted to plan a spa day. Sage made a note to revise her 21-

day guarantee and privacy policy on her website before heading back into her room to change into her gym clothes.

A few days later, back in her home office and attempting to focus on work, Sage was confused when Pierre showed up at her door. Curious as to why he was there and unannounced, Sage swung the door open and crossed her arms under her chest.

"What are you doing here?" she asked.

He frowned. "We were supposed to have breakfast today right?"

Sage's eyes widened before she shook her head. "After what happened? You can't be serious."

Pierre frowned a little at Sage's clipped tone. He had been leaning against her doorway, but now he was standing up straight. "I was, but judging from the tone in your voice we have a problem?"

Sage laughed. "Pierre, do you not remember how our last conversation went?"

"I do," he nodded. "We both said some things that weren't too professional, which is why I let you cool off. Now, I'd like to take you to breakfast so we can talk and get back on track."

"I don't think we have anything else to talk about."

"You don't think we have anything to talk about? Not even us?"

"You fired me, Pierre."

"Exactly," he said. "I fired you from being a contractor for my company. I didn't break up with you."

"I don't really see the difference."

"You can't think it's the same. You aren't that dumb."

Sage's skin felt hot. "First you fire me and now you're calling me stupid? You are out of your mind to think I want to go anywhere with you!"

"I didn't call you stupid," Pierre sighed, running his hand down his face. "That's not what I meant and you know it."

Sage closed her eyes and exhaled. "I don't think there's anything left to say."

"So you're willing to throw away something good because I bruised your ego at work? You really don't see the problem with that?"

"If you don't respect me as a consultant, as an equal person who brings value to your business and to your life then yes, I am willing to throw it away because it wasn't that good in the first place!"

Pierre frowned. "Wasn't that good? Never picked you out to be a liar, baby."

Sage rolled her eyes. "Yeah, well...you don't know me as well as you thought you did."

Pierre scratched his head as his shoulders dropped. "Why are you like this?"

"Like what, Pierre?" she asked, dryly. Sage was over this conversation.

"So damn defensive."

"I'm done listening to you tell me everything that's wrong with me. If you aren't apologizing for how you treated me, you can leave."

Pierre's nose flared as he nodded. "Alright...you got it."

A few days later on the other side of town, Julian was finished going through the reports Sage provided. He was curious about her numbers, so he'd been in the office all weekend, going over last year's fuel reimbursement receipts, matching them to the loads they corresponded with. He triple checked them, knowing he'd have to be thorough when he brought the confirmation of Sage's findings to his hard headed cousin.

"Can't wait to see him look goofy," Julian joked.

"Are you in here talking to yourself?" Nicole asked, rounding the corner of his office door. "You're here early."

Julian looked at his watch to see that she was as well. "Wanted to catch up on some things before Pierre got in."

Nicole nodded, smirking as she looked around the office. Julian fought not to smile at her lingering. "Do you need anything?" she asked.

"If you could get some coffee going that would be great."

"Already on it," she said.

"That's good for now then," Julian ignored the pout on her disappointed face as she turned to walk out. He was aware of Nicole's little thing for both him and Pierre. Although he was attracted to her, he wasn't up to playing the game of which Harris man would win. They'd done enough of that in their younger years.

However, Julian was sure his cousin wouldn't be looking at another woman for a while. He had seen the transformation almost as quickly as it happened. Julian did not believe in love at first sight, but watching Sage and Pierre was like watching one of those corny romantic comedy movies. He didn't like the idea of his cousin being caught up with a woman so quickly, but if he was being honest, Pierre could do a lot worse than Sage. Way worse.

Convincing him of that was another story.

Julian caught up on some other things while waiting for Pierre to get in. There were some bids in his inbox for their construction team that looked promising, so he scheduled times to go check them out with his project manager. He worked on his government proposal for a little while until he saw Pierre pass his door.

"Cousin!" he yelled, knowing that irritated him. Pierre appeared at the door within seconds.

"It's too early for you," Pierre said. "What's wrong?"

"We need to chop it up," Julian said, waving his hand towards the chair in front of his desk. Pierre sighed as he walked in and sat down.

"I don't want to talk about Sage," he said.

"Too bad. She's right."

Pierre frowned. "What?"

"I used her formula and went through last year's numbers," he said. "She's right, P."

"You triple checked?"

Julian rolled his eyes. "You heard what I said. So go ahead and call her to apologize."

"Nah," Pierre said, instantly. "Even if she's right. She didn't handle that professionally. I should have never tried to date her, especially not while we were contracted."

"You're not wrong," Julian said. "But now it's over, apologize and continue dating her."

Pierre frowned. "You think I want to be with a woman who wants to argue with me all the damn time?"

"I think you're exaggerating."

Pierre shook his head. "If you want to apologize to her so bad, you do it. Send it with a bonus or something, I don't care. As far as us dating though, that's over with."

Before Julian could protest, Pierre and his coffee mug were back out of his office.

Fourteen

Sage smiled as her grandmother's face came into view on her screen.

"Granny, who did your hair. Those are cute!" she said. Granny ran her hand over the top of her braids and smiled.

"Thank you, baby. One of those girls at the church did," she said. "She's been so fascinated with my hair she said she wanted to braid it."

Sage laughed. "Well, that was nice of her. How are you feeling otherwise?"

"Enough about me," Granny said. "I called to see if you got your mind together about that man."

Sage frowned. "Londra called you?"

"Don't matter," Granny said. Sage made a mental note to kick her sister when she saw her. "What matters is you need to go make that right."

"Granny," Sage sighed. "It's not going to work."

"Have you been listening to the sermons I've been sending you?"

"Yes ma'am," Sage said. "But I don't think God would want me to change who I am for a man, Granny."

Granny shook her head. "Did I say that? Whew chile, you do jump to conclusions."

Sage ran her hand over her face. "Well, that's what he wants. He wants one of those quiet girls who lets her man order her food for her. Might as well cut it up and feed me like a baby while he's at it."

Granny laughed. "You sound like your momma. Tell me exactly what happened."

Sage told Granny about how well she thought their date went and then how he blew up on her in the office and fired her. She even told her about how he showed up at her place.

"So y'all issue was mixing business with pleasure."

"Granny, I want a man that I can do business with. How am I supposed to help my man build a legacy if he won't let me?"

"Was that what you were doing?"

"That's what I was hired to do," Sage said, correcting herself. "He needed my help saving his business."

"You said he didn't want to hire you in the first place, right?"

Sage shook her head. "His shareholders weren't happy with the lack of increase in profits."

"Anyone ever come and told you how to run your business?"

Sage sighed. "Granny it's not the same. It's literally my job to do that."

"Is it your job to do it with sass and condescending tones? Your delivery is horrible, baby. Like now I can tell you want to go off on me like I won't slap you back into your childhood," Granny said, laughing. Sage kept quiet. "Sage, I'm very proud of the business you're building, but you have to know that you'll catch more flies with honey than with salt, baby girl."

"Why do women have to be docile and sweet all the time? Why can't we be assertive and confident."

"Anyone can be assertive and confident," Granny said. "But none of us should be smug, judgmental, and cocky. You didn't like when he was in the beginning now did you?"

"No, I didn't," Sage sighed.

Madie gave her a calming smile. "I get it, baby girl. You want to be the strong one. You always were, but I can tell from when you came up here that you're tired of that."

"I am," Sage whispered.

"Well stop it," Madie said. "You can be a strong woman and not be stubborn. No one asked you to do that."

After being checked by her grandmother, Sage felt a little defeated. It seemed as if everyone in her life was telling her that she was wrong for standing her ground. She had even begun to second guess herself until she received the apology from Julian, confirming that she was right along with a bonus payment. The fact that Pierre hadn't reached out with that information was not lost on Sage at all.

Even with all of her anger about the situation, Sage missed him. What he called arguing was a welcomed challenge to Sage. She loved that she could have deep discussions with him and they could voice their opinions and points and see each other's sides. It didn't make sense to Sage, because she felt that after their initial issues, they fit well. However, Pierre wanted someone docile and meek and that wasn't Sage. If he couldn't see what he was losing then she wasn't going to help him find it.

Fifteen

Julian Harris had enough of his cousin mopping around the office like he'd lost his best friend. He had been annoyed about everything. Julian had to take lead on showing Philip his error and going back to redo the mileage. They decided not to make any of the driver's pay for their past mistakes, but he did put a newsletter together to explain what would happen going forward. Now that business was handled, he could focus on getting Pierre and Sage on the same page.

Julian knew that after Pierre's last conversation with Sage, he didn't plan on reaching out to her again. Being the concerned cousin that he was, he decided to not mind his business this time. Not sure how receptive Sage would be to him reaching out about their personal life, Julian tried the next best thing.

After locating Sage on social media, he found her best friend, Carmen's page. They had only met at the company bbq, but she had a cool vibe and Julian figured she would be down to get Sage and Pierre back together. He looked over her profile for a moment, realizing how attractive she was. It looked as if she worked in some sort of healthcare field and Julian had to admit that she filled her scrubs out pretty nice.

Shaking his head to get his thoughts off her body, he clicked the **Message** tab and waited for the window to pop up.

Is your girl as miserable as my cousin is?

Since she wasn't active, Julian closed his browser and decided to call it quits for the day. He was going to a few construction sites that following morning, so staying late in the office was not an option. Pierre was already gone and Julian thought Nicole was too until he saw her in the break room, cleaning up.

"You know the crew comes in a few days?" he asked, throwing his trash away. Nicole jumped a little at his sudden presence before nodding.

"I know."

Julian smirked. "You got plans tonight?"

Nicole turned to face him directly and sucked her teeth. "Julian, don't act like I haven't tried to get up with you several times."

"I'm saying, I'm trying to see what's up with tonight?" he asked, smiling. Nicole rolled her eyes but he could see her trying hard not to blush.

"Whatever, Julian."

"I'm being serious right now," he said, throwing his hands up. "But if you aren't with it…"

Nicole rolled her eyes. "What did you have in mind?"

Julian smiled before telling her to call him once she got settled at home and he would come by. Nicole agreed and Julian headed out of the office. He checked his messages and smiled.

She definitely is. What are we going to do about it?

Julian nodded, going to his Instagram to find the promotion he was looking for. Pierre and Julian planned to go to a

108

fundraiser gala that a local promoter was holding for cancer survivors. He took a screenshot of the flyer and sent it to Carmen with the discount code that he used to get their tickets. Carmen sent back a smiling emoji and said she would make sure Sage got there.

"Now that my work is done," Julian said, driving out of the parking lot. "Time to play."

Sixteen

On Sage's birthday, she decided to do something different. She usually went all out, but decided to spend it as a self care day instead. She had been running thin for the last few weeks. Now that she was in between clients, she just wanted to destress from life and start over as best as she could.

True to his word, Donovan Anderson showed up in St. Louis for Sage's birthday. He offered to take her to lunch on that day, but Sage opted for the day after. She was meeting him at a new black owned restaurant in the central west end. Since she was relaxed from her spa birthday, Sage was open to have the necessary conversation.

Despite her reservations, Sage smiled when he walked into the restaurant. Donovan was average height for a man, deep caramel skin with salt and pepper waves. Sage always loved her dad's smile, so when he flashed it at her, she felt like a little girl again waiting for her dad to come home at the end of a workday.

"There's my oldest angel," he said, pulling her out of the booth to hug her. She groaned.

"Please don't call me old."

"Two more years to 30," he teased. Sage rolled her eyes as they both sat down.

"I ordered you a sweet tea," she said. Donovan frowned.

"I actually need it unsweet," he said, waving for a waitress. "I have to watch my sugar."

She frowned. "Is something wrong?"

"Just being cautious," he said. "I'm getting up there in age while I'm talking about you."

Sage smirked. "We both better watch it then, huh?"

The two made small talk, catching up as they waited on their food. Sage had to admit it was good talking to her father, but she was anxious to see if he would address the elephant in the room.

"How's work going? Your sister tells me all about your consulting company."

"She does? Oh...well, it's going pretty well actually. Just finished up with a client."

"That's good. I'm proud of you."

Sage sighed. "...Thank you."

"I wanted to see you in person to have this conversation. Your sister seemed more receptive to me being in her life after all that happened with D, but I noticed you aren't too happy with me."

Sage frowned. "Honestly Daddy, I'm not. I feel like you left us all and it was already hard enough dealing with Demetrius being gone."

"I lost my only son, Sage..."

"And Alondra and I lost our brother...Mommy lost her son, too...Granny lost her only grandson. We all took that loss. We were supposed to take it together."

Donovan scratched his head and sighed. "I know. You're right."

Sage sat back in her seat. She was prepared for more excuses and blame on someone else. She hadn't prepared for him to say that.

"It hurt," she finally whispered.

"I'm sorry," Donovan said. "I didn't deal with it like I should have. I had no one to blame except that kid who pulled the trigger. He was in jail and I didn't feel any better. Nobody taught me how to deal with those types of emotions," he said. "Never had to...The only choice I felt like I had was to block it all out. I know now that wasn't the right choice. I lost my marriage behind that, but I can't lose my daughter. As your father...I'm asking for your forgiveness."

Sage wasn't sure where the tears came from, but letting them out felt good. She wanted to argue. She wanted to point out more things that he had done wrong. She wanted to vindicate her mother and the rest of their family. However, all she could hear was his sincere apology and sit in that moment.

"It's going to take some time," Donovan said. "But we'll get back to where we were."

Sage looked into her dad's eyes and nodded. "I promise to put in more effort." Her words caused his shoulders to relax.

That moment clicked for her. It wasn't always about being right or placing the blame on someone. It was about what you valued as important, as a priority. It was about what you fought for. Being able to accept that apology was big for her, just as she knew being able to give it was big for her father. It made Sage think of Pierre. She wanted to apologize to him for cutting him off when he reached out to her. However, at this point she was sure he wouldn't hear it.

Seventeen

It had been a few weeks since Sage had spoken to Pierre. She thought she would have been over him by now, but she found that wasn't as simple as she hoped it would be. She missed him. She missed working with him, seeing him so passionate about his business and standing his ground when he thought he was misunderstood. She missed talking aimlessly for hours and cooking with him. Sage even missed arguing with him.

She was angry. How had she created so many memories with this man in less than a month? How had he gotten under her skin so much in so little time? It wasn't fair that she was forced to get over something when she wasn't even sure what that something was in the first place.

Sage couldn't even focus on getting ready for the charity event she was attending with Alondra and Carmen. She was shocked when Carmen not only invited her, but purchased her ticket. It was for a good cause and since Carmen's grandfather had passed away from cancer, Sage knew it was important that she support her friend. It would also be a great networking experience.

Sage opted for a strapless, gold gown with a corset top. The satin fit around her hips and fell down to her heels, a split showing most of her thigh. She felt a little daring with her heels. The snakeskin open toe had a strap that wrapped around her calf. A classic finger wave hairstyle with natural makeup and a clear gloss on her lips pulled it all together.

Alondra, who decided to drive, called to let her know she was outside.

"You are showing out with this leg out!" she said, tapping Sage's thigh She laughed.

"I did a little something," Sage said.

"I know this is a bougie event, but this open bar is about to turn it up."

Sage shook her head, laughing at her sister as she sent Carmen a message to let her know they were on the way.

The gala was in one of the banquet halls at Ameristar Casino and Hotel. It was fun walking through the building, seeing people watch them and wonder where they were headed. They took the elevator up to the second floor and it looked like a different place. The decor was very elegant and everyone upheld the dress code. Sage and Alondra met Carmen outside of the ballroom.

"Do they do this every year?" Sage asked.

"Apparently so," Carmen said. "This is the first time I've heard of it."

"Who told you about it?" Sage asked.

"...Oh, there's the bar! Come on." Carmen pulled Sage and Alondra to the bar to get their first round of drinks.

Once they found a table that had enough space for the three of them, Alondra sat down while Carmen and Sage went to network. Sage had already seen a few people she knew and wanted to speak. However, she had the feeling that Carmen was up to something.

"Best friend," Sage said.

"Hmm?"

"What are you not telling me?"

"What makes you think I'm not telling you something, Sage?"

"You keep looking around. You know someone in here?"

Carmen looked behind Sage and her eyes got wide. "Oh crap, okay so Julian told me about this event and he and Pierre are right behind you."

Sage almost choked. "What?"

Carmen turned Sage just in time to see Julian smiling with his arms out.

"Look who it is? What's up, Sage? Nice to see you Carmen."

"Heyyyy, Julian," Carmen said, hugging him. "Hey Pierre. Sage, what are the odds?"

Sage eyed her. "I'm going to kill you."

"You ladies look nice," Julian said, looking at his cousin to see if he would say anything. Pierre just smirked.

"Sage."

"Pierre."

"Oh geez," Carmen mumbled. Julian said something to her but Sage couldn't hear it over her frustration.

"That's it?" she asked. Pierre finally made eye contact with her and smirked.

"Didn't you tell me to leave you alone?"

Sage sighed. "Pierre, I…"

"…Right," he said, turning to Julian. "I'll be at the table. They'll be serving dinner soon."

"I cannot believe you," Sage whispered, walking back to the table with Carmen. "Why would you do that?"

"Sage, just go talk to him."

"Did you not hear how he responded?" Sage sat down and took Alondra's drink.

"Hey!"

"Pierre is here," Sage said. Alondra sat back in her seat.

"Oh, what happened?"

"He's being rude as hell...again!"

"In his defense, you played him when he tried to reach out to you," Alondra said.

"Exactly!" Carmen agreed.

"Both of you...be on my side right now," Sage said.

"We are and that is why we are telling you to apologize to that man."

"For what? Are y'all forgetting how he all but threw me out of his office?"

"You both handled that wrong," Carmen said. "But is it worth throwing away what you were building with him?"

Sage huffed. "It was only a couple of weeks."

"That has nothing to do with how you felt."

Sage sat back and took a sip from the glass again. She scanned the room, finding Pierre a few tables down doing the same but looking at the band in the front of the room. She thought about all the time she spent with him outside of his office and how comfortable she was getting to know him. How his business practices challenged her own and made her want to do more with her business. She hadn't felt wanted in a genuine way since her relationship with Troy. She hadn't even been opened to it until now.

Carmen and Alondra were right; she didn't want to let that go just yet.

Throughout the dinner and ceremony portion of the gala, Sage went over her apology in her head like a work presentation. When she saw him head to the bar once the band started back up, she took her chance.

"Can we talk?" she asked, stepping next to him at the bar. Pierre sighed before turning to her.

"You want to talk now?" he asked. Sage nodded. "About what?"

"Us."

Pierre frowned. "According to you, that's dead right?"

Sage sighed. "I said that. I thought I meant it, but I don't. I miss you and if you still want to talk about moving forward I'd like that a lot."

"I don't see how you want that now? A week ago you were all but cussing me out."

"Well, you did put me out of your office. Let's not forget that," Sage shot back. Pierre sighed, taking a sip of his drink before standing up from the bar stool. Sage bit her lip as she fought against the sensation to cry. Pierre stood tall and confident, just as he had when they first met. Sage knew, however, his confidence wasn't in her.

"Sage," he sighed. "I just don't...we wouldn't work out. I can't do this everyday."

"Do what?"

"Argue with you. You never let your guard down. You never let me have the last word. I need a woman who wants to work with me in life, not against me to always prove she's right."

"That's not fair," she said, her voice cracking under the pressure.

Pierre sighed. "Maybe so."

Without any more words, Pierre picked his drink up from the bar and began to walk away. Sage looked towards where she knew Carmen and Alondra were watching and frowned. They motioned for her to go after him.

"What?" she mouthed, throwing both hands up.

"Go apologize!" Carmen mouthed.

"Get your man!" Alondra threw in.

"Pierre, wait!" Sage said, trying not to cause a scene. He sighed as he turned around. "Just wait...hear me out, please."

"...Okay."

"You're right," she said. That caused his facial expression to soften. "I know. I don't like to admit when anyone else is right but me," she chuckled. "But you are. I am combative and I'm stubborn and I don't take opposition well and up until now

119

that's the way I've run my business and it's worked for me. I realize now that..after meeting you, it hasn't worked for me in life."

Seeing his shoulders relax a little, Sage took a chance and stepped closer to him.

"You challenge me and you call me out on my BS. I thought you didn't respect me…"

"I do respect you," he said, his tone softer than it had been since they began talking.

Sage smiled softly. "I know that now. We were too much alike in ways I wasn't prepared for. I see so much in you that I've wanted for so long but I was afraid to let myself admit that I deserved it. I am absolutely all of those things you said, but I'm willing to move the needle for you. I don't want to argue with you. I want to build with you. I want to help you continue building your legacy because I believe in it. I want to be with you...and I think you want that, too."

The event moved on smoothly around them and Sage felt like she couldn't breathe. She felt her temperature rise from anxiety, waiting for a reaction. Three weeks ago it would have been easy for her to let him walk away, it would have meant nothing to her. Any good sense she had completely changed her mind. Their chemistry, their vibe was something she wasn't willing to give up.

"Anyone ever told you that you'd be a great lawyer?" he asked. Sage looked up from her thoughts just in time to see him smirk as he began to move closer to her. Her heart settled as she smiled, feeling his strong hand grip her hip.

"So I've heard," she said. "Is that a…"

Pierre cut her off by placing his right hand on the back of her neck and pulling her into a passionate kiss. She sighed, feeling her body relax against his. It felt amazing. He placed both of his hands on her face and guided the kiss, slowing it down but increasing their passion.

He pulled away, holding her head back so she would need to look up at him, but she hadn't opened her eyes.

"I'm sorry I put you out of my office," he said before kissing her again. Sage nodded in acceptance of his apology. "Look at me...I'm not trying to change you, Sage," he said, looking into her eyes. "As your man, I just want to help you grow."

She smirked. "That sounds like change...but change is good."

Pierre laughed while shaking his head. "Couldn't help yourself, could you?"

Sage wrapped her arms around his neck while looking into his eyes. "When it comes to you? Nah, I can't."

Pierre kissed her again as their friends finally joined them.

"Congratulations on getting over yourselves," Carmen said, handing them both a glass of wine.

"Didn't take as long as we thought!" Julian said. Alondra agreed and the three of them laughed as Pierre and Sage looked on with straight faces.

"Oh wait guys, I think they're mad," Alondra said, pointing at them. "It's all love."

"Don't sound like love to me," Pierre said. "What you think, baby?" he asked, leaning down to kiss Sage's neck. She tried to keep a straight face but blushed anyway.

"I think you're right, babe. They sound like haters."

"Now they're going to agree on everything," Julian said, rolling his eyes.

"We'll agree to leave y'all," Pierre said, grabbing Sage's hand. "Let's dance."

Sage giggled as she followed Pierre to the dance floor, vowing to herself to let him lead.